Idle Grounds

Idle Grounds

KRYSTELLE BAMFORD

HUTCHINSON
HEINEMANN

HUTCHINSON HEINEMANN

UK | USA | Canada | Ireland | Australia
India | New Zealand | South Africa

Hutchinson Heinemann is part of the Penguin Random House group of companies
whose addresses can be found at global.penguinrandomhouse.com

Penguin Random House UK,
One Embassy Gardens, 8 Viaduct Gardens, London SW11 7BW

penguin.co.uk
global.penguinrandomhouse.com

First published 2025
001

Typeset in 13.5/16pt Garamond MT Std by Jouve (UK), Milton Keynes
Printed and bound in Great Britain by Clays Ltd, Elcograf S.p.A.

The authorised representative in the EEA is Penguin Random House Ireland,
Morrison Chambers, 32 Nassau Street, Dublin D02 YH68

A CIP catalogue record for this book is available from the British Library

ISBN: 978–1–529–15458–0 (hardback)
ISBN: 978–1–529–15459–7 (trade paperback)

for my dad,
James William Bamford,
who was curious, kind, and found
humour in depressing situations

Always we all have need of Zeus.

Aratus, *Phaenomena*

Foreword

The following is an account of an afternoon in June in which we sallied forth, and then, for the most part, back. By *we* I mean the cousins, who were a varied crew with the normal range of grubby characteristics, and while we weren't great, I'd like your sympathy because of our humanity and also what we've lost.

As illustration, please take the Russian Imperial Family:

Unlike us, the Romanovs were a good-looking bunch, which is not always the case with the idle rich. Not the mother so much, but the rest of them were nice to look at, with abundant, free-flowing hair and rolled-up sleeves and an air of happy mischief. There are photos of them freewheeling at the Winter Palace with bare feet and silly hats and giant fake teeth. In one, a daughter peers out from a single bed shoved in a corner and you have the feeling she's got a bad cold, and her mother sits next to her, telling her a story or something. In another, the littlest Romanov, who couldn't even get a paper cut otherwise he'd die on the spot, is wearing a sailor suit and looking nervous around a sheep. They fly-fish and stand on each other's shoulders and hold hands. They look like they spend a lot of time in each other's company, and though they may have had their complaints, it seems, all in all, like *an extremely nice life.*

The dad was czar for twenty years before they were shunted along, and that's when the very bad things started to happen, including lots of chores done at gunpoint in the snow and much worse. It doesn't bear thinking about. Then, after some time, they were all shepherded down to the wall-papered basement of a house called The House of Special Purpose, and it took ages for them all to be killed, just *ages*. It was a mess.

What I imagine is this: doing anything for twenty years makes you feel that you can keep on doing it indefinitely. And, of course, nearly everyone's assumption had been that they would. Keep at it, that is. Though if you really want to take a wide-angle view of the thing, it wasn't actually twenty years but twenty generations, and in any case it was long enough for it to have always been that way as far as everyone was concerned, and then, suddenly, it wasn't. If you look at kings from the same period, they all had identical eyes and facial hair because they were cousins, and you really have to wonder how well they slept at night.

Anyway, the whole thing makes me tremendously sad. I hate looking at photos of the Winter Palace gang because, despite their failings, they seemed nice and funny and like they had hobbies and frustrations and loved each other very much. And because it wasn't a once-in-a-lifetime portrait sort of thing but neither was it a selfie plucked from thousands, they had to keep the ones where some people were looking away and some were just out-and-out brooding and some looked surprised. It was the right number of photos with the right amount of significance attached to each one, so the record we have of them, if not perfect or complete, is a variegated one. *Vibrant* is maybe the word, which comes from *vibrate*, something that moves.

So it was an awful tragedy. A horror.

But still, if you think about it, a really big part of the horror is that they had names and also that we can see pictures of them doing this or that, daydreaming or being bored or closing their eyes: things that make us think 'hey, wow, that's us!' Also that they just weren't used to it, that kind of treatment. It went against the grain. It's the shock of the thing, is what I'm saying, and my new and somewhat untested theory is that when something is shocking, it also seems unfair even when it isn't. A shock disrupts the normal flow of things, and what is normal usually feels the same as what is fair, and I guess what philosophy and history and all sorts aim to do is to prise these two things apart – what is normal from what is fair – but only ever after the fact. Only, actually, when it's too late for the people involved.

And what that means is that somewhere in the backs of our brains, as we're pouring our cereal or examining a bug bite, we feel that there are people who are used to that sort of malpractice, and so, when their end comes, it isn't really sad because we feel that it's written into the chart of their lives. And because it's not shocking that these people had really awful things happen to them, it's also not unfair. It is what it is.

3

In short, it's hard to be sad about someone being dead when they were never really alive in the first place.

Who's ever shed a tear for a nameless serf? Have you?

Who are you?

1. Initial Sighting

As always with these things, it started with a birthday party. What you should probably know is that the day was bright and clean even though it was summertime, which was malarial at best most years, but this year it wasn't.

As I said, it was bright and clean.

An aunt with yellow, highly styled hair had baked a cake, also yellow, with sugar confetti. It was a boxed cake rather than a homemade one, as those are a variable lot and not to be trusted. Her name was Frankie. It was Frankie's house but not Frankie's birthday because she wouldn't have baked her own cake, even if it was just from a box, nor would she have hosted her own party, as it takes a special kind of person to do that and Frankie was just ordinary in a hysterical, wet-eyed kind of way. She was unmarried and also the only Republican in the family, as far as we knew.

It was one of the grownups' birthdays; it doesn't matter. What matters is that we were all together, which everyone seemed to dread and anticipate in equal measure. Cars and cars and cars rolled up Frankie's blue-gravel drive and every last one of them nosed forward the last few feet, and you just knew they were saying something like 'Well, here we are!'

Cousins stuck their legs out from the car doors, always the children first, parents girding their loins behind the steering wheels.

'It's eleven now; we're out of here by three,' our parents said, a fount of shaky determination, 'three at the latest.'

Cousins eyed up cousins, standing a full cousin-length away, giving a shy wave while the adults eased themselves out with a dish covered in tinfoil or a six-pack of Beck's tinkling like a piggybank.

'Stay up here, OK? Up where we can hear you.'

Chickens hopped around on hostile yellow legs. Bug spray was passed along, hot dogs were sliced from their packaging. Hummingbirds appeared at the feeder, fed, vanished.

Frankie had built the house herself. She'd built it so far back from the road that you forgot leaving was an option. Though technically within the borders of the town where most of us lived, Frankie's house was really in horse country, and although it was only ten minutes in the car from the elementary school, horse country had hardly any people in it. Instead it was full of split-rail fences and birch and pine woods and a few old houses landed like dice rolling way off the playing board into their own shaded grottos for ever.

It was very pretty.

The house's back deck dropped away into a sloping pasture in which Frankie kept two horses whose names, it seemed, were always changing. Beyond the pasture with the horses was the bulk of the woods, which tumbled downwards to a river that was mentioned sometimes but never as a destination. The river was, as far as we knew, the boundary of the family property.

On the wall of Frankie's dining room she had copies of oil paintings of hunting parties, or that's what we guessed anyway because of their red coats and trumpets. The horses looked absolutely panicked, the people on their backs panicked too, but in a more focused way. No one ever ate in there, in Frankie's dining room. We just passed through it on our way out to the deck, or from the deck into the dark of the house to use the bathroom or to get ourselves a glass of water or fetch something from our parents' coat pockets. Once the adults had a drink in their hand, everyone relaxed. Back then the bottles were green for the most part and in the sun they looked unbelievably expensive, like they were carved from something you had to excavate and polish.

Anyway, what I've established, I hope you'll agree, is that it was a beautiful day and there was no reason for what happened to happen. Nothing propulsive in the atmosphere or setting. The adults were talking about many things; they had known each other for so long the conversation just rowed across the surface of the water like this:

'Reagan is worse. Mom would have loved him, though.'

'Mom would have left Dad for Reagan if Dad hadn't left first, no question.'

'Reagan would have loved Mom.'

'She would have died before voting for him, though.'

'Yes. Do you remember when—'

It was interesting in that we were excluded entirely, but after a while we got restless and went inside where there were some more of us sitting on the steps that went up to the bathroom and bedrooms, and this lot were talking amongst themselves like birds before they fly off in one jaggy but coordinated movement. There were ten of us cousins, give or take, and the tallest and also the oldest one was Travis. He was twelve. He looked at us with his long swinging jaw, trying to weigh us up. Time had passed since the last time we'd all been together, his face said, but blood was blood.

'Do you guys want to see something?'

Yes, we said. We always want to see something.

We all went up the stairs together. The wallpaper had both stripes and flowers, so either the flowers seemed caged or the stripes looked like they had some kind of bacterial infection.

'OK.' Travis pressed his finger against the screen of the bathroom window. 'Look.'

What we were looking at was Frankie's front yard and drive, with our parents' cars, and then beyond that, at the far-left periphery of our vision, a shed with Frankie's tools and behind it, the band of woods that separated Frankie's house from her neighbour's house, which used to be the house they all grew up in – our parents, that is – their childhood home.

'Just watch.'

It was funny, because even though we'd been to Frankie's many times, our parents had never really mentioned the childhood home. It was there under a weight of trees like a bug under a rock and so we'd never given it a second thought. Until Frankie told us, we hadn't even known they'd lived there, but here's what we did know: sometimes our grandmother, Beezy, had whumped them with a switch cut from a blackberry bush.

We watched. If Travis weren't so tall and old, we would have given up watching, but he pressed his finger against the screen so hard it turned violet-white and then we saw it. One of the flock from the stairs gave a little moan.

'What is it?'

'Shh.' It was certain Travis's finger would be grated right down to the knuckle. The blond prow of his hair nosed against the screen.

At first it was just a movement, like when you close your eyes in the sun and things jump about. From the wall of trees hiding the childhood home to Frankie's shed. A ten-yard dash.

'What is it?'

'Shhhh—'

Oh, it was fast, you had to give it that. So fast you just knew that whatever it was it didn't want to be seen, but the thing is, we had seen it.

'There!' Travis was in a special school.

One of the little ones was standing on the toilet seat and nearly toppled onto the rest of us below, but Travis hardly noticed. His whole body was like when you rub a balloon on your hair. At Travis's school there weren't any desks, just beanbags, and a robotics lab and a theatre where you could sit all around the stage so no one ever needed to feel left out. The Macalasters' kitchen was filled with mugs with the school's motto on them, which were the words *nostra sponte* underneath a shield with animals and plants. It was costing his parents the earth.

Frankie's yard was still in the sun, pinned down by the heat. Directly below us, in spitting range, there was a statue of a pop-eyed jockey with his face painted bright paintbox pink that our parents hated – just get rid of that thing, oh my God, in this day and age. He stood at the mouth of the blue-gravel drive, holding a lantern – which must have been intended for someone else, he had no use for it himself – out towards Frankie's shed and the thicket of pines, with the childhood home lost somewhere behind it. And this thing moving so fast, the size of a big cat, 15 per cent bigger than a big cat.

Last Thanksgiving, Travis's mother, Aunt Maureen, had slapped Frankie across the face. We were all there at Aunt Maureen's, but we hadn't really been paying much attention until the moments just before the slap, which was so hard we felt slapped ourselves. Frankie had cried and smiled at the same time and Aunt Maureen had said, 'Sorry, I'm sorry,' over and over again until someone took her into the other room, and no one saw her until board games later that night where she didn't play but just sat there, Travis's dad rubbing her back in circles.

Zip zip zip. From the treeline to the shed but not back again, that was the part we couldn't figure out: it was just ever in one direction. You could be excused for thinking that meant it was many different things running to the shed, but we just knew it was the same thing over and over, which was worse, somehow, even though it should have been better that there was only just one.

The door rattled splenetically at our backs, but it was just an aunt-by-marriage, needing to pee.

'What are you all doing in here?' she said, and we shrugged.

'Come on,' Travis said in his quietest voice, and crooked his finger towards Frankie's bedroom.

Frankie's bedroom had a thick aquamarine-ish carpet and potted ferns and a statue of a woman made of white marble, no bigger than the smallest of us. Her face was like 'O!' and she was so soft-looking you might want to run your hands all over the stone, except for the snake that wove itself around the folds of her body. Its head reared back at a vicious angle, which let you know that it was a biting snake, as opposed to, say, a talking one. Otherwise it was a quiet room, full of pet hair.

We crowded to the window.

We didn't know what to hope for: thing or nothing. Thing meant that our day, only somewhat extraordinary, would become truly remarkable, but it would also mean that whatever else we feared – a woman sewing us into our bed while we were asleep, for example – was possible, even if it wasn't probable. It opened things up in ways both surprising and permanent. Nothing, on the other hand, meant that we would need to go downstairs eventually and get ourselves a 7-Up, start thinking about the nine times-tables or something along those lines.

That or listen to our parents, who always ended up talking about one thing, which was what had happened with our grandmother, Beezy, and who was responsible and what the roots of it were and who was responsible for the roots. Everyone with invisible pickaxes and miner's lights and dirt all over the place. Shining lights into each other's faces, getting careless with their pickaxes the more they drank, not being mindful of the dirt or who got dirty.

We heard our aunt flush next door and, just as we all looked at the sound, there it was, like it sensed we were distracted: zip!

It was clever. It already thought it knew us well.

And it was just then, sparked by the flush, that the littlest one, whose name was Abi, made a break for it. Abi was Travis's sister and she was nice – you could tell, even though she was only three, the type who kissed your elbow when you weren't looking. She'd always been that way. The other thing about Abi is that she had a purple cast on her wrist on which someone had done a tic tac toe and her pigtails stood straight up from her head, which made her look like a satellite floating in space and gave her an aura of alert melancholy. She still took naps in the afternoon, but when she was awake she was everywhere. In many ways she was the best of us.

Abi was out the door and, we had to presume, down the stairs, but honestly here is what it looked like: when she rounded the corner and out of sight, it looked like the house moved towards her rather than, you know, the other way around. It looked like the house just jumped and snuffed her out.

Travis reached towards where she'd been and called 'Abi!', and what was funny is that he was scared for no reason. You could tell that he was really terrified. We all were. The house spasmed, then sat back.

'Hey, Abi!'

But Abi was gone as if she'd never been there at all, and there was nothing we could do, so eventually we resumed watching the stretch between the shed and the treeline that shielded our parents' childhood home, and it was our stretch now, whether we wanted it or not, and even from Frankie's bedroom we could feel the warmth of the springy soil coming up through our soles. We felt the sky was preternaturally blue, but otherwise, otherwise the day was bright and clean.

2. Basement

No one knew where the jockey with the lantern came from, but Frankie had so many things like that and, even as a kid, it made you stop and think about the journey. First, you had to imagine someone wanting to make it and then someone wanting to buy it. Then you thought about someone deciding to keep it and then pass it along, saying, 'Here, this is for you, I thought this reminded me of you,' and then on and on, and the more hands it passed through the harder it was to say, 'No! Please! Do not think of me, forget me entirely.'

But she liked it, Frankie. She liked the jockey. What she said was that she saw nothing wrong with it whatsoever and also she thought it was cute. Frankie claimed to be a child herself, which was why she didn't have any children, so what that meant was that one day the jockey was coming to live with one of us. It was travelling towards us at an undetermined speed, though which one of us would be chosen it was impossible to predict. Only the fact of its arrival was certain.

'What are you kids doing up there?' It was one of the uncles, too lazy to come up the stairs. He'd been tasked, it was clear, with finding out what we were up to so the adults could wash their hands of the whole mess later on if it transpired what we were up to was bad.

'Nothing,' Travis called down, and we nodded, yes, that's right, that's an absolutely brilliant answer.

'Allllri-ight.' And just like that his voice was gone. We could hear his presence take itself off, back to the deck, and with it our resolve.

'I want to go downstairs,' one of us announced.

'Me too,' another said, just for something to say.

'Not me,' a third chimed in.

This was a shambles of the highest order. Travis's big teeth looked exposed. The little woman with the snake stood next to him and, upon second thought, the snake must have also been a talking one – you could tell because the little woman looked like she was being told something cloak-and-dagger.

'Alright,' Travis said finally, tucking his teeth behind his lip, 'alright, just hold on one second.'

He went back to the window.

Travis looked and looked some more, and then he traced his finger against the metallic fibrousness of the screen and here is the sound his fingernail made: screeeee. It was so rash it took our breath away. It was a signal, surely, to the thing at the treeline, or at the very least an inadvertent beacon, an accidental missive. But when Travis turned around, we could see he had done it because his mind was elsewhere. He was thinking about something else entirely. His eye, you could say, was off the ball.

'OK,' he said, and he put his long hands in his shallow pockets, 'let's go downstairs.'

We bunched at the doorframe, no one liking to be first, or worse, last.

'Come on.' Travis sighed when he said this but it was a gentle one.

We popped out the other side of the doorframe in one lump sum and went down the stairs, often holding hands. The wallpaper blooms loomed.

One time by accident, one of the aunts slammed one of the cousin's hands in the car door and the cousin reported, *post facto*, that a flower had sprouted on the back of their hand, as big as a cabbage and the same colour as their skin, which was bluey peach. They had watched it, they said, while they screamed, but later on it wasn't there anymore and someone had said it was a delusion, which was probably correct. That's what the wallpaper looked like, a delusion.

At the base of the stairs we scanned left, over the dining table Frankie had set with big white plates with gold edges that our mothers said were dust-collectors, to the bright square of deck. From where we were standing you could see a distracted and hairy red leg.

Blooms loomed is an internal but not external rhyme. They are fraternal twins or, better yet, sororal twins, because those words are girls rather than boys, there's no doubt, or neither or both.

Frankie had only gone to secretarial school but loved poetry and what she loved most was 'The Charge of the Light Brigade', which she said was about being brave in the face of adversity. One Christmas she taught us the words and here's the part I remember because it's short and rhymes externally quite a lot:

Theirs not to make reply,
Theirs not to reason why,
Theirs but to do and die.

When we'd finished the grownups clapped loads and Frankie hugged our faces with her hands and cried like she does.

'Hmmm,' one of the cousins said now.

Another cousin traced a circle on the floor with the toe of their jelly sandal, then stared into the middle of the portal they'd just fashioned.

'Why don't you guys go,' Travis suggested, 'onto the deck. I think Frankie put out Cheez Balls. If you don't run quick, Abi will have eaten them all by now.'

This put the wind in our sails. Several of us made for the deck whether we liked Cheez Balls or not. What we were after was the thrill of the chase and also the chance, maybe, to have our heads stroked by a parent, just to check in and say hello even for one minute.

The grownups were sitting down and standing up, some in very deep shadow and some in sunlight and some in both, making the parts of them in sunlight seem realer than the bits in shadow. Beyond the square of deck there was the barn's gable with its single window, like a third eye or something equally horrible, staring out over the paddock and down the long wooded slope that contained, somewhere at its base, the river.

'Oh, stop it,' someone said, down the neck of a bottle, then louder into the open air, 'just stop it already.'

'Easy for you to say.'

'Wo-o-oaah there, girl. Come on now.'

Conversationally the grownups were stuck in a door-frame and waiting to be popped out the other side, but our arrival wasn't enough of a shove. It didn't do a thing, actually, but there was a plastic barrel of Cheez Balls on the table and so we helped ourselves. The shadows were so cool and refreshing, like rock pools. No one got their head stroked, though. We just scattered between legs, gathered our Cheez Balls on paper plates, and retreated into the house where Travis was getting himself a glass of water from the tap. He was wearing a polo shirt with fat coloured stripes and a white collar, which made him look like a formal caterpillar. He took a drink and offered to get us water, and we all drank from glasses that said 'Coca-Cola' on the side.

'So Abi didn't get all the Cheez Balls? That's good,' Travis observed. He stuck a pinkie in his ear and moved it around.

'Abi wasn't there.' It was Autumn, who was seven and the bearer of all bad news.

Travis extracted his finger.

'What do you mean?'

'Abi wasn't there.' Autumn liked to string things out. She was the kind of person who would pull a loose thread on your sweater and say 'Hey, you have a loose thread.'

'She wasn't on the deck?'

Autumn shook her head, extremely pleased.

Travis put his glass next to the sink and went out

through the doors to the bright square. We could hear him say something like 'Yeah, uh, it's pretty good', and we guessed that Travis had been asked about his very special school because the family was tremendously valedictory about the whole thing. They never let an opportunity pass. And then he came back in.

'Abi?' he called out, medium-loud. 'Abi?'

Because Frankie's house was built by Frankie, it was actually quite basic, like a doll's house. It had a bottom and a top. We knew Abi was not at the bottom because we were there now and it was essentially one large room with a staircase going up the centre. And we knew she was not at the top because we had just been there.

Travis went to the kitchen window and watched with his bony face, but this time he was careful not to make a sound. This time he kept his hands in his pockets like he was covering their mouths in a movie.

'What do you see?'

Travis shook his head back and forth, which meant 'I see nothing.'

'Maybe she's in the basement,' one of us suggested.

Travis turned away from the window and shrugged.

'OK,' he said, 'let's look.'

Most doors to basements are flimsy, I don't know why – they're the absolute worst doors in the house. In happier families, they have a calendar or something on them, maybe some takeout menus in a clip strung up on a nail. They are used, is what I'm saying, for something other than leading down into the ground where no one ever actually wants to go but are only ever forced to go, by a storm or an even greater necessity like this one. It's possible they're so thin because the basement wears at them.

Travis stood at the top of the wooden steps – the type without risers that make sensible people absolutely sick – and called Abi's name. His voice bounced down the stairs and out of sight. He reached up to the little chain above his head and pulled, and the lightbulb became beautifully yellow, and that's probably the colour all people should wear when they get married. When Autumn's mother, Pin, got married, practically nobody came and she wore a navy suit and a ferry tooted its horn just as they were about to say *I do*. It was a funny wedding, everyone said at the time, we found the minister asleep on a log and when he woke up, he pulled his tie from his shirt pocket. A sad wedding, actually, is what they meant. Afterwards, everyone had clams.

Travis went first and we came down behind him.

'It smells like a dog's butthole,' Travis said to himself, and we gasped and also fell in love.

The problem with light is that it only spreads so far. We could see a washing machine and cardboard boxes but we couldn't see what was in them or behind them or in between them.

'Abi,' it was Autumn this time, self-appointed second-in-command, 'are you hiding from us? Come on, Abi, don't be afraid of us, OK?'

It was a stagey performance and here's why: Travis's mother, Aunt Maureen, had agreed to look after Autumn and her brother five afternoons a week for the whole summer while Pin worked in a plant nursery, hence Autumn's assuming such a central role in the search – she wanted to prove herself useful and not a drain on family resources, even though it's not your fault if your parents divorce. Everyone wants you to know that right away; it's the first thing they tell you.

Perhaps but not definitely this was the reason she was such a pain.

'Abi!' we all called from our little yellow island, 'are you here?'

Travis stepped off into the dark, which swallowed his ankles and then washed right up his back.

We watched him. He walked over to a corner and rattled some boxes and then some chairs, lacquered like a fancy mirror, where instead of a reflection all you saw was cloth. The cloth had a pattern of flowers with stripes to match the wallpaper, though you could only see it if you moved the chair a certain way in the light – the pattern flared up and then flattened back into the cloth, which is called damask. Damask feels like the perfect name for something that hides, just like heirlooms sounds like hair-looms, which is also rather pretty grotesque.

It was Beezy's furniture. Some of it, anyway.

'I don't think she's here,' we said hopefully.

Travis walked from corner to corner, craning his skull.

'Sometimes she won't listen,' he said, 'when she's mad.'

We knew this. Not about Abi but about ourselves. Now that we thought about it, we probably didn't know Abi at all.

Beezy's furniture was part of the whole thing with the slap and the recurrent pot-stirring that was happening upstairs. Beezy had inherited things from her *own* childhood home, which had been located somewhere back there in the woods not far from where we were now, although it wasn't there anymore. After Beezy got married, the things lived for a while in our parents' childhood home, next door past the trees, and when she died they went to Frankie. All three houses were in roughly the same area because Beezy's family used to own a lot of land. It might help if you imagine them – firstly Beezy's childhood home, second our parents' childhood home, and third Frankie's house, which we were in now – as nesting dolls taken out one after the other and then you burn the first one down.

One of the things Frankie had inherited was the statue of the little woman and the big snake.

'It has a presence, don't you think?' Frankie had said once to Travis's father, and Travis's father had said, 'It sure does.'

When she was first married, Beezy had been a teacher because she loved literature and wanted to share it with young people.

'Why did she stop?' This was last Thanksgiving but before the slap.

The hours were so long on Thanksgiving. Sometimes someone played the piano and sang about Nuclear War, which made it even longer, so we asked questions to pass the time.

'Well,' Frankie's eyes filled, 'I think she was just too good for them, Scout's honour, that's what I really think.'

We'd been eating celery with peanut butter and raisins, which were called Ants on a Log. During this, the very longest section of the day, in which we weren't allowed a normal lunch because we were *saving ourselves* for the main event, there was nothing else for kids to eat. Just some blue cheese and walnuts. After dinner Frankie always presented Beezy's favourite, mince pie, which sounded inscrutable. Like us it just sat there, its little pastry leaves wilting across its forehead.

'She had Uncle Andrew,' Travis's mother, Aunt Maureen, said over the last part of Frankie's sentence. 'And also she hated kids.'

'Oh, you.' Frankie touched Aunt Maureen's arm and smiled.

'Well,' Aunt Maureen put her arms in the sink up to her elbows and started scrubbing; the pots and pans shifted around in the hot water, shedding the food we didn't want or need, 'it's true.'

Frankie frowned.

'Beezy loved children. She had five!'

'But did she want five?' Aunt Maureen and Frankie had forgotten about us. To them, we had fed and vanished.

'Oh, Maureen,' Frankie laughed, as if this were beside the point. In between bites of Ants on a Log, we considered for the first time that it was possible to have children you might not want. Anyway, I think that was the first time we considered it. I can concede that some of us may have considered it before.

'Right,' Travis said after a while. 'Let's go.'

The kitchen was huge after the basement. It was like the light from the windows made second windows on the floor and counter. We stood in the sun and waited for Travis to formulate and then offer a plan. He pulled at his lip.

'I'm going to look for her outside,' he said. 'You guys stay here.'

'No!' Autumn again. 'We'll come with you.'

Autumn had the most beautiful long black hair, it really fell down her back like Japanese waves on a greeting card. Besides surprising speed, it was her only good quality.

'Nah, honestly, you guys hang back.'

I will say, though, that Travis looked nervous, and this sent a tremor of sympathy through the flock.

'Yes,' we said, imagining ourselves linking arms and progressing across the lawn or maybe in a circle so no one could get picked off the end, but that would entail some of us walking backwards, so maybe not. 'We will come with you.'

'Well,' Travis touched the doorknob and then his hand jumped like oil on a griddle, 'OK, if you're sure.'

'We are, we are,' we said, and fell into line. As we prepared our bodies and thoughts, the deck doors slid open and a grownup went to the fridge and took something out, humming, then left again. It was as if we didn't exist at all. It was very strange and wonderful. We took a breath. Travis's hand grasped the doorknob and pulled and all we could see was sunlight.

3. Chicken Coop & Barn

We did not go left towards the shed and the treeline, no we didn't. We went right.

'She didn't go that way,' Autumn said, glancing at her wrist and then at the treeline behind the shed. 'No way, José.' Pin had given Autumn a digital watch at the end of the school year and she was wearing it now. It was white-and-black checkerboard pattern with some coloured squares thrown in for a party atmosphere and Autumn had developed the habit of consulting it even if the question wasn't related to time.

The sun was like sun reflecting off metal but coming to us direct. It was that bright. We looked left to where Autumn meant, mostly blocked from view by the large, comforting bodies of our parents' cars. Was it zipping now, in the open air that we shared with it? Who could tell? That it had been zipping was enough for us to stay away, even if it was taking a break, even if it was sleeping it could always wake up.

Travis pulled his lip which was dry – you could see it now that we were outside.

'Well . . .'

We were standing between the railroad ties Frankie used to mark the footpath through the flowerbeds. The railroad ties were heavy and reddish, bulwarks really, and we were loath to part with them. The jockey stood next to us as we deliberated, only up to our belly buttons. He held out his lantern and smiled, which made him pathetic because it was daytime.

'OK, we'll go this way first.'

We went right, under the kitchen windows and below the deck, which hovered above our heads like a magic carpet with our parents on it. One of them laughed, and it was Pin and it was what they call a steely laugh. The shadows of the house were the black sails of sailboats, meaning that the side of the house was the ocean's surface and we were walking on the sky, maybe even along the horizon. Frankie had built these steps, also with railroad ties, and they went down and around the house, under the deck, and out of sight. Travis let us go first because actually the danger was behind us, you see.

'Abi!' we called. Down here the deck formed a ceiling and the light made the wood a greenish colour and the ceiling creaked under the feet of the grownups like the sound green wood makes when it expands.

'Abi?'

There was a scream. It was someone who'd gotten down and round the corner. Their scream was also like green wood, expanding. Travis parted us and ran down the steps and we filled the vacuum he'd left behind at breakneck speed.

'Abi—' Travis was panting in fright, his hands on his hips.

It was a little one and they were pointing at a chicken.

'What the shit?' Travis placed a hand on their head. 'That's just a chicken.'

'Chickens is scary!' the little one said. They weren't wrong. This one was black and huge and had red wobbly bits coming off its head. What was spooky was that it wanted you to think it was soft but really it was sharp. It lunged its head to the ground and raked a toe across the gravel.

'This chicken won't hurt you, OK? OK? Let's go look by the coop and you'll see they're just a bunch of old, dumb birds.'

The little one skirted around the chicken with their paws drawn up under their chin. They didn't take their eyes off that chicken for a minute, but the chicken didn't care. I think the chicken didn't even notice, if you want my honest take. It just moved in the sun, heavy in its feathers, looking for bugs. We pressed on.

The chicken coop was next to the barn, which was painted the same colour as Frankie's house, blue with white trim, like the house's brainless twin. When we walked past the open barn door its whale-mouth called to us but we did not heed it. Not yet.

The chicken coop did not match anything and it was huge, two storeys. Frankie had built it herself, and if you looked at it sideways you realised that most of it was old cupboards and wardrobes tipped on their sides and nailed together, their doors hanging down their faces like they'd had a stroke. It stank like chickens, which was par for the course, and straw was everywhere. Chicken wire separated us from the structure. Its pattern was hexagonal and so it looked very organic, like it had grown there instead of being made in a factory and stapled into place. The door was open so the chickens could come and go as they pleased. The place was an absolute ghost town.

'Abi?' Travis called at the coop. 'Um,' he looked around, 'I think I'm too big. Does any one of you want to go in?'

We quailed.

'OK,' Autumn said. She pushed forward her little brother, a skinny guy who didn't say much, 'he'll go.'

Everyone agreed he was a top-notch candidate.

'Look,' Travis crouched down and put his hands on the little brother's shoulders, 'we'll be right here.'

The little brother nodded. He had bags under his eyes and legs like pick-up sticks. His name was Owen.

Owen was wearing a red t-shirt that said 'I Won Big at Majestic Sands' across the front. Travis held the wire door all the way open and Owen crouched through.

'Good boy, Owen,' Autumn said, but it was mostly for us, to show off her encouraging nature.

Owen looked back at us from beyond the hexagonal veil, the skinniest chicken who ever lived, and then hunched his way up the plank and disappeared into the closest hatch. We waited.

'What birthday is it today? I can't remember.' Someone just passing the time. No one said anything. The trees were so tall, taller than usual, like clouds pouring out a column of black rain.

'Owen?' Travis called. 'Is she in there?'

No word from Owen.

'Owen?' Autumn called. 'Abi?'

If we lost two of them there would definitely be trouble. It would be like the time we used our sneaker as a grappling hook to snare our other sneaker that was sinking in the pond and then lost our grip, both sneakers meeting the same watery fate. They call this good money after bad.

Pin was very recently divorced from Uncle Carl, who was just Carl now because he was out in the world with no connection to us and also he never saw his kids, who were Autumn and Owen, and when someone asked her if she wanted to marry someone else, this is what she said: 'No sense throwing good money after bad.'

'OK,' Travis got down on his knees. 'I'm going in.'

Just as he said this, Owen's face appeared at the hatch, a pale oblong against all that stinky darkness.

'Owen!' Autumn seemed really relieved and, for a brief moment, we liked her more than we had.

Owen said something indistinguishable and then disappeared back into the coop.

'Owen!' Autumn flew through the door and up the ramp and we followed like all those animals in the Bible – no one wanted to be left behind outside the wire, just like no one had wanted to go inside the wire alone. We were brave in groups only, except for Owen.

The coop was dark except for occasional slices of sunshine and the smell was out of this world.

'Owen?'

We found him in the last compartment, which was also the darkest. We had never seen anyone make themselves so small. Autumn scooted forward on her knees and touched her brother's shoulder and, like she had pressed a lever, his arms shot out and in each palm there was a little skull, but they weren't skulls. They were eggs.

'Put them back,' said Autumn.

Owen shook his head. His hands closed around the eggs.

Something had come over Owen.

'Knock it off, Owen. Watch it!' Autumn was pissed off. Oh, she was furious now that she wasn't scared anymore. 'Owen, give them—' She made a grab.

Owen did a half-tuck roll and a shiver went through us all. We imagined the eggs mashed against his Majestic Sands t-shirt, but when he unfurled there they were, twin moons in the coop's planetarium, which would make Owen a planet and us planets as well, though less significant ones. His commitment was clear and Autumn relented, calling him a birdbrain, which was correct: that's what he was now.

There were so many of us in there it was hard to see how we were going to get out.

'OK,' said Travis, 'everyone move backwards.'

And so we did. We were an organism moving backwards. When the last one was out, we blinked at the high-noon sun and then looked at Owen, who had his two eggs, and a feather stuck to his shorts. He would not look us in the eye.

'Hmmm, so no Abi,' Travis said, not caring about the eggs.

'No,' we said.

'Can I hold an egg?' one of us asked, but Owen shook his head. Out of the coop the eggs looked blue and very heavy and beautiful. No one could blame him.

Travis looked around.

'Barn?' he said, and we said, 'Sure.'

The barn door was closed when before it had been open, and there was something wrong with its rails. Everyone except Owen put their fingers right into the crack between the door and frame and lifted. While we strained, Owen stood back with his eggs, ginger and nervous because he had to be careful, of course; he was a mother now.

We lifted with our knees but no dice.

'Hm,' Travis said, 'OK.'

If we stood three of us on each other's shoulders, then we might have been able to try the runner at the top of the barn door, but there was no need. We walked round the side of the barn, into Frankie's barn office. The office had a desk and an old maroon-leather rolling chair and a garden of fat satin show ribbons growing from the wall. Next to the ribbons there was a telephone and a telephone book and a chalkboard covered in Frankie's handwriting, which looked like the trail of a plane in freefall, and an electric light that was designed to look like an oil lamp but otherwise it was junk. There was nowhere to hide and, for that very reason, funnily, we wanted to stay. We liked it in there. Frankie's office smelled like when you dig a hole and also like drying grass and also of breezes and shadows.

On our left there was a flight of stairs up to the barn's loft and on the far wall there was a door with a fluted-glass window. The window gave a hazy picture of the other side: the horse stalls heaped with hay and a rail of stiff blankets and the great hinged feed bins with their heavy metal scoops hanging on brass hooks, but the door was locked so that was that. Travis rapped on the window and shouted Abi's name, but all that happened was that his breath made everything go opaque, like someone was holding up a sheet of white paper from the other side of the glass, or like the room was full of the sort of snow that seals you in and poisons you with gas. We pressed our ears to the door but there was just white noise.

Someone made a joke about Frankie not wanting the horses to make emergency calls and we moved on.

'Hey,' Autumn said, pointing to a photo on the wall at the foot of the stairs, 'it's Beezy.' And there she was, Beezy sitting on the stoop of our parents' childhood home with the three aunts and two uncles as children in stiff shorts and short-sleeved button-up shirts, their black-and-white faces scrubbed clean. Aunt Maureen, the Boys, Pin and Frankie, in order of preference. Beezy was smiling, her face turned to the side. She was wearing a narrow skirt and her dark hair was rolled up in curls at the base of her neck and her hand rested on the slender skull of a silky, baleful-looking dog, with another similar dog coiled on her feet like a huge tasselled shoe. The children who were our parents looked happy and busy, as if they'd been asked to stay still for just the minute it took to take a picture and then they were off again, building boats or playing cowboys or whatever children of that era did with their time that was so great. To the left of the photo there was a tall shadow, and those were the pines that separated the childhood home from Frankie's house. Only now Beezy's family was on the other side of them, probably just a few minutes' walk through the woods, if one were so inclined, though one generally wasn't. Especially not now, of course, because of whatever we'd seen from Frankie's bathroom window.

'She looks pretty,' Autumn said in a shy way, like Beezy could hear her, and we all agreed that she did.

You might be wondering why we didn't know much about the childhood home, but here's the thing: our parents hid the true nature of the house from us for so long that it was obvious to even the dumbest amongst us (Autumn) that it made them sad. And kids, despite obliviousness to many things like etiquette and social cues, are hugely in tune with sadness, especially their parents'. And what did our parents have to be sad about? Lots of things, it turned out, though it's possible they were overly sad, which is called being maudlin. Or maybe they were sad about all the wrong things; that was possible too. They were sad about politicians and people they once knew who were dead or had changed so much they might as well have been dead, about parking restrictions, library closures, and more private sadnesses that we had no access to. But when they were together, the thing they were sad about was Beezy, and what they'd lost when she'd disappeared into the hospital and what they never had in the first place. That was the way they talked about it. It wasn't just that she had died in a senseless way, or that years before she'd landed in her wheelchair and then her husband had gone off. Instead, it was like those things had travelled backwards to infect all the stuff that had happened before, all the way back to their births and before that even, and everything tasted a little bit like sadness in the way that you can't just cut a mouldy bit off a tomato because it's all water. That's my working thesis anyway, which I may revisit in the fullness of time.

'Euch.' A cousin squatted on their haunches below the picture and pointed a finger at the floor.

No one touched it because no one knew what it had been. A scrap of meat, though most horses are vegetarians – glossy and near-black and the size of a stamp, the kind of thing we imagined filled mince pies. There was a little smear off one end like a comet's tail.

'Our cat used to put dead birds on our pillow,' another cousin mused apropos, I suppose, of seeing meat where it shouldn't be.

We looked again at the picture of Beezy.

The stairs let into a very big and open space, which was the loft, and contained everything for every season and occasion and worry. We looked, and while we did not find Abi, this is what we found: a smashed bird's nest, a rack of clothes that were mostly things with lots of buttons, a box of women's shoes with square heels, a Filofax in handwriting that was not Frankie's, a chainsaw, a wooden sofa with no cushions and a high back, a mountain of hay bales, brown paper bags full of

Christmas decorations, a book about golf and another one of jokes, a red accordion file of what grownups call *papers*, and about a million other things. In the middle of the floor there was a hatch.

'That's so you can throw stuff down,' Travis said.

'What kind of stuff?' we asked. We imagined Frankie opening the hatch and showering the concrete floor below with high-necked shirts, the shirts twisting in the air.

'Hay.'

We stood on the closed hatch door. We could feel the living animal of its potential thrum under our feet, but at that moment we had bigger fish to fry. We would come back and throw hay down the hatch. The promise of it smouldered in the distance.

Because Beezy had died on her sailboat when Travis was very small, none of us but Travis had ever met her. 'When was Beezy's birthday?' we'd asked the grownups a while ago, and were told that Beezy hadn't celebrated her birthday, not since she could help it. It was a foreign concept to us, not celebrating your birthday, though I suppose when someone dies they become all their ages at once so it doesn't really matter.

As we made our way down the stairs, we could feel the enormity of the loft sealing itself behind us, and as we passed Beezy's picture at the foot of the stairs, we wondered if she hadn't been looking right whereas now she was looking left at the black blur, which was the pines. The children who were our parents were still staring at us with their shiny foreheads, so that was good at least; that was good enough for now.

4. Paddock & Rose Arbour

What I should have said is that there were no horses in the barn. At the time it didn't feel necessary – you could have simply assumed from my not mentioning it – but actually it's worth being explicit that the horses were not in the barn because they were in the paddock directly behind the house. The horses were black, with their necks bent at unnatural angles like articulated straws. From our position in front of the barn, we were close enough to see the bluebottles circling their rumps but not close enough to see the ones settled near their eyes. In the centre of the paddock there was also a single broad tree of thick and indeterminate verdancy behind which someone could hide, no problem.

Some of the cousins were under the impression that they loved horses but no one, it turned out, was keen to go into the paddock and here's why: the main and only thing they tell you about horses is don't stand behind them, but standing in front of them isn't great either. Horses' teeth are like dentures but on a very surprising scale.

'Maybe she's behind that tree,' some genius piped up.

The thing is, there were lots of trees, any one of which could have a small child crouching behind it, a world of trees, infinite in number and variation, spreading further and further away from the house down towards the river in an uncontained spillage of green and damp black and moth brown. However, if you were to hide behind one tree and one tree only, that would be the one.

'Stay away from the horses,' Travis said, and we fell into formation.

Frankie had been talking about giving us riding lessons for years.

'Hey!' she would say, nearly every time we saw her, 'you know what would be neat?'

And when our parents would shake their heads no no no, Frankie would help us beg them. She would even call them Mom and Dad, even though both her parents were dead:

'We'll be safe, we promise, Mom!' she would plead, one arm around us, pressing her cheek up to ours as if we were one and the same.

'Look at her legs,' our parents would say afterwards, 'legs aren't supposed to look like that.'

And it was true. Frankie's shins were slick with purple and red scar tissue from being thrown and dragged by frightened horses.

The horses lifted their long heads at us in tandem. They weren't black at all, it turns out, but eggplant-coloured as much as anything. They looked like collapsed silk tents. Their eyes were bright and gave very little away.

'They're wondering why we were in their house,' Owen whispered, cupping his eggs against his chest, and Autumn said, 'Shut up, Owen,' and someone sang 'Hello

Operator' until they were told to shut up as well. And then we were all quiet except for the grass, which rattled around our ankles, and the bugs, who hummed.

Before she wound up in her chair, Beezy was a horsewoman.

'She was a first-class horsewoman,' Frankie told us once, 'she was hunt secretary in her day,' and she'd looked off into the distance and made a gesture with her hand like she was unmooring a spider's web.

'Didn't you ride?' we'd asked our parents when Frankie brought up lessons, and our parents shook their heads like *not for lack of trying*, and it turns out that none of them rode horses when they were small, not even Frankie. Frankie, Aunt Maureen said, had taught herself when she was older. She'd thumbed for lifts to work as a stable hand at a riding school the next town over – mucking out stalls, filling buckets, shining up tack and the whole shebang.

'But what about Beezy?' We just couldn't understand. 'She was a first-class horsewoman!'

We pictured our grandmother as young as our parents in her cinnabar jacket and bullet-shaped hat, hurtling through the scrub – *halloo*. Our parents just laughed and then they said 'Beezy was Beezy', which meant absolutely nothing to us, apart from Travis maybe. One story the family liked to tell was that, when Travis was christened, Beezy sent him a reproduction wooden Dogon ceremonial mask from the Crate & Barrel catalogue that measured four feet long, and her other gift was that she did not attend the christening.

This year, we were under the impression that Frankie's horses were named Odin and Blondie.

'Hi Bloadie! Hi Ondin!' Autumn called across the grass, and one of them stayed still and the other one let the names run the full length of its body. 'Oh, I mean, hi Odin! Hi Blondie! We're just looking behind your tree, OK?'

We crossed the field and the horses lifted their heads and turned their large eyes on us. When we got to the tree, we could see that there were no children behind it except for us, and it's as if we all agreed we didn't qualify as children anymore but were instead something else entirely.

'What's this?' Someone pointed to a filament twanging in the sunshine.

'Yuck, here's another one.'

And there were more, there were dozens of filaments and, if you followed them upwards with your eyes, you could see that each one was attached to a branch and, if you followed them down, you could see that each one was attached to the ground like a circus tent. And why we saw the filaments first I don't know, because for every filament there was a large, black caterpillar curling hideously above our heads, and what I hate is they want you to think they have hair and two eyes, but it's not hair or eyes, and in fact they're not like you at all in any way.

'Euch.'

Maybe it was because we were so badly outnumbered but when we turned to look back at the house for reassurance, we could sense suddenly and very sharply that our parents were out of earshot. We could see them there on the deck, hanging off the side of the house. They were close enough so we could see them gesturing to each other but we couldn't hear a word and so, of course, they couldn't hear us either, and the bugs and the grass started up again in an extra-loud tenor and it was very much like when a big bully stands in the way to let a littler, nastier one set to work without anyone spotting what they're up to. Like that exactly. It was our first mistake or at least our most recent.

The horses, whatever their names were, started walking backwards, just a little hop-shuffle, and the grass purred and the filaments bowed to an invisible hand, twanging.

'Abi?' Travis shouted suddenly, and his panic was dark and straight as pencil lead, and it went right through us, and we all started lifting our feet because I don't know why. Because we wanted to lift ourselves up onto a very tall platform and look down at whatever was in the grass through the sights of our rifles.

The horses didn't like this and now they didn't like us either. They started to dance up on their legs and shake their rubbery faces at us and the grass rushed around under their hooves. Oh, it was sick. They weren't close to us but at any moment they could be as close as they liked, which was the second problem with horses. They were, it must be said, *transformed*.

Owen was holding his eggs up in the air, stock-still, his gaze fixed on something in the grass and his mouth working a little but weakly. Then he spun around on his heel and ran, clutching those eggs, true as a plumb line towards the horses who were hauled right up on their rear ankles, lips drawn back. They were mad in the old sense of the word and also the new. There was an almighty goulash of legs and wild movement and a good spray of screaming from our side and the horses just came down and down and down again with Owen curled like a caterpillar right under their hooves and we saw him in our mind's eye get smashed open like he'd been dropped from a very great height and then ground into paste, trod right into the grass. That's the world our brains wanted us to imagine, with ants stuck in his blood and little fragments mixed in. And then Travis was there, the hero of our collective story, and he reached out one long arm and pulled Owen from the melee with legs crashing like typewriter keys, and then they were free and away and back under the fence from whose perimeter we were now watching. Travis touched every part of Owen, felt his head like a melon, looking for splits and gouges and breaks. Autumn was on her knees feeling Owen too, and us all crying out, 'Owen, Owen, are you OK, Owen!' And here's the thing: even though his chest was fluttering and his eyes were trained on the thing which was gone now, Owen was perfect. Even his eggs were intact.

'Oh, Travis,' Autumn said, and pointed, and actually it was Travis who was hurt. A deep scratch like a badly drawn X marked the back of his calf and there were beads of blood sewn along it, but Travis didn't even look at it because he had grown in both stature and valour.

Travis stood up and scouted at the house, with his hand flat above his eyes like a man looking out at a prairie for signs of the enemy or a cool drink. As we admired his profile against the blue of the noon sky, something came back to us, something we'd overheard Aunt Maureen say earlier that very day to one of the aunts-by-marriage regarding pastures anew. We looked at Travis and saw what she meant. Travis was a shiny bugle raised in the air. He was our man on a penny fresh from the mint.

Travis looked at Owen, who was still on the ground. 'Owen, do you want to go back?'

Owen used his elbows to push himself up a little without compromising his babies and he shook his head *no*, and then Travis did a couple of thoughtful stretches with his hands on his waist and then nodded *fine*, as if our recent brush with death had pushed us past the threshold of language, even though, as you'll see in a moment, it hadn't.

It's not uncommon for people to assume that Beezy was in a wheelchair because she'd had some sort of tragic fall from a horse or whatever, and in fact that's what we assumed for many years, to the point where we hadn't bothered to ask. But what happened was this: Beezy got sick. Sickness is less romantic but also less your fault, so it evens out in the public eye. Sickness is a blanket draped over your cage. It was a stroke, and for some reason we thought she had it while doing something hugely athletic, but actually she just had it while doing something average like sitting around. It was Pin who found her, and Frankie, the youngest, who called the ambulance, and it took Beezy months to come back from the hospital, and maybe she never really did; that's what the grownups liked to say, 'But did she ever really come back?', like it was a new thought every time. She was, I think, not even fifty.

We dusted ourselves off and did not look at the horses directly, but could see out of the corners of our eyes that they had gone back to eating and were no longer looking at us with resentment but something more akin to armistice mixed with conceit.

'Where do you think Abi is?' we asked.

Travis was too kind to say that, if he knew, we wouldn't all be looking like this, like maniacs falling off and under things. He pulled his lip. The X on his leg had smeared into a red triangle, so you would have never known it had been a letter at all. In Travis's room at home there was a string of nautical flags that spelled 'Travis Downe Macalaster' if you knew how to read them, which Travis did, explaining that the first flag in the string – up-to-down red, white and blue stripes – stood for *T* but also meant *Keep Clear*, so what I'm saying is that Travis was very comfortable with secret messages. The hair on his legs was weird and bushy because he was twelve, which was a chink in his armour for sure, but you can't love a hero without faults. He was limping slightly.

When we started towards the rose arbour, some of us were holding hands and some of us had our hands loose but swimming in the air, looking for a mate.

The rose arbour was on the opposite side of the

house to the deck and what no one wanted to say was that our parents were, at least for the time being, lost to us. The roses climbed the hill until they met the gravel drive where our parents' cars were and the shed and the line of trees, and so the other thing no one wanted to say was that we were circling round inexorably towards it: zip zip zip!

When you're an adult, roses are filled with portent: loving, being loved, being extremely attractive, etc. The particular roses above our heads, on the other hand, were huge and dying and odorous. They were cream, pink and orange, and all of them eaten a little with rust, their stems and leaves near-black. As we climbed the railroad ties we thought about them dropping down on us, their rotten perfume in our hair and clothes like a relative who never gets hugged in their nursing home.

When we reached the midway point of the arbour, we realised, of course, that Abi was not here either and suddenly we were struck by the thought that we had assumed Abi would be in a defined *place*, like the barn or the coop or the paddock, when in fact she could be in no place at all. We were thinking too much like ourselves and not enough like Abi who was perhaps, it was dawning on us, a subtler kind of person. The kind of person who would hide behind an awkwardly placed chair or at the corner of a house, where the ground dips below a passer-by's sightline. Liminal spaces. This was our first hint that we would not be artists, not one of us, but instead would go on to do a range of things with more rigidly defined parameters of success and failure. Do you remember when you first knew? I bet you must. For most people it happens older, but for us it was at this very moment in the rose arbour and whether that was a blessing/time-saver or what it's really impossible to say.

'But that doesn't mean you can just take it.' This was Aunt Maureen, and it was Thanksgiving on the Year of the Slap. It was after dinner and we were in the *sitting room*, which is what Aunt Maureen called her living room. The adults were on couches and chairs, which she called settees and wingbacks. There was a fire in the grate and we were in front of it, watching its colours waver and shift because there was nothing else to do and on each side of the fireplace there was a pie-faced china dog and, tucked in beside one of them, a standing rack with all sorts of implements for poking and prodding and also some milk-coloured rocks they must have found at the beach and thought were so great they simply had to take them home. We were eating chocolate turkeys.

What Aunt Maureen didn't like was that Frankie had taken the statue of the woman and the snake, even though no one else wanted it – as with the jockey, everyone thought it was awful.

'And it's not just that. No one else stood a chance. You just swooped on down.'

'But I didn't.' Frankie's voice was awfully quiet, the voice of a person crossing a tightrope between two very tall buildings.

'Excuse me? I missed that.' We liked Aunt Maureen, as a rule, but today she seemed engorged.

'There wasn't anything in the house—'

'Sorry?' And now it was clear that Aunt Maureen had understood what Frankie was saying but was going to make Frankie repeat it until she came to regret and relinquish her point.

'There wasn't anything in the house that meant something to you, so I took it. I took it, Maureen, because it meant something to *me*!' Frankie brandished a finger, tears in her little eyes. Her emotions had over-expanded greatly, they were rubbing up against each other and everyone else, and because they left room for nothing else, the air around us went right up the chimney – we could feel it rush past, nearly taking us with it.

'Fabulous.' Aunt Maureen was standing up.

'Maureen,' Aunt Maureen's husband Uncle Steve said, but Aunt Maureen was not up for listening.

'It was me,' Frankie was saying at the same time, 'it was me all the while and now you—'

'Gee-golly, so you're her *tillerman*, Frankie, you're her—'

'Maureen—'

'Just, no, Steve, I'm saying this – of all the—'

'It was me, Maureen, it meant everything and now you—'

Etc etc.

When the slap came it was like one of those roses, if you want to think about it that way: the head was Aunt Maureen's palm and the stem was her angry wobbling arm, as well as the three firm steps across the sitting room she took to reach Frankie's face, which was the flowering, I guess, when it bursts out of itself and everyone looks at it and can recognise and give it its generic name. Frankie put her hand up to the spot on her cheek where Aunt Maureen's hand had been as if she wanted to treasure it, and Aunt Maureen reached out as if she wanted to take it back.

'Oh God, I'm sorry.' Aunt Maureen did a half-turn, her hands opening and closing. 'I'm sorry, Frankie.'

It was a terrible moment and while terrible things are usually interesting, with this one the interest had nowhere to push through, it was that densely woven. We all looked at our feet and hands.

Uncle Steve had led Aunt Maureen away and Frankie stood there with her hand on her face, smiling like a coin underwater.

'Look—' One of the medium-sized and discountable cousins was holding something between their fingers. Roses hung around their head like a newly sprung god, and they held it with distaste so we could all see. It was a hair thing, pink, an infinite loop with a plastic star hooked on to each side, and from it, a single hair shining against the very brightness of the day, because of course it was Abi's hair: it couldn't have, at this juncture, been anything else.

5. Cars

It was a clue. The clue was that she had been here but she wasn't anymore. It was the kind of clue you're always getting, in that it didn't help us very much at the time but later assumed a really disproportionate significance. Travis held the two stars in his palm and then tucked them in his pocket.

We stood in the sun and looked up the rose-covered incline towards the drive and the shed and the treeline in front of our parents' childhood home. You might be wondering why we hadn't as yet investigated the area between the shed and the treeline, but if you are, then you know nothing about fear.

'We could check the cars?' Autumn suggested.

We looked at Travis. The summer before, Travis had spent ten days at space camp in Washington, D.C., and rumour had it that he may have gone into an antigravity chamber. He nodded and so we turned back to Autumn and said, 'Yes, OK, fine.'

The cars were the last line of defence between us and the thing at the treeline. They were for the most part gas-guzzlers, station wagons and Jeeps, huge up on their wheels, with grates on their faces like muzzles. On a normal day we wouldn't have thought about them twice but today they seemed fantastic, like war elephants or war pigs, depending on the make. A selection of war animals. The uncles told us once that the Romans set pigs on fire to scare their enemies' elephants, but we weren't planning on anything like that today. Today size was enough, so we climbed in and out, in and out, never looking out the windows. If we'd looked out the windows while we were inside the cars, we could have seen pretty much anything crawling around on the gravel. It would have known, of course, that we were suddenly close, our legs dangling from open doors, and so we didn't dare look out the windows at all. What we did see (not Abi: Abi wasn't there) was a bottle of peach nail polish and a leather day planner the size of a Pop Tart and a baseball hat squashed past all recognition and some pennies and nickels but nothing larger. We checked Frankie's car last because it was the most vulnerable and therefore the least appealing: a toothpaste-green two-door with the top down, like a sailboat without a mast. The windshield was framed in silver and just asking for someone to put a rock through it. It was, besides her horses and Beezy's old stuff and her sense of utter self-reliance, Frankie's most prized possession.

Frankie's car was a car of tragedy. Here's a story: Frankie had a friend who was a mechanic. The Mechanic was an unusual friend for Frankie because Frankie was a terrific snob, but there you go. I have no idea how they met, probably he was fixing up Frankie's car and they just got to talking. Anyway, he and Frankie used to pal around. The Mechanic was short and round with a moustache, and he was, everyone agreed, a really good guy. He was the sort who would just show up when you needed him most, empty-handed but otherwise eminently agreeable. One night a handful of us sat on the hood of Frankie's car and looked at the stars and the Mechanic showed us the Big Dipper, and it was the first time we'd heard of any such thing, if you can believe it. We were that small/dumb. He held his thumb up and closed one eye.

'There,' he said, 'there it is.'

We all looked up, trying to see the same thing together – it was the first time we'd considered the heavenly bodies.

So the Mechanic got squashed when a car he was fixing up fell right on top of him. Something wasn't right with the hoist and Frankie wore black for a month and she wouldn't look at you when she talked to you, like her eyes were boats only tied very loosely to their dock.

It wasn't Frankie's car, of course. That would have been ridiculous. It didn't matter, though, because her car had the Mechanic all over it anyway. What I'm talking about is memories.

We scoobied up and into the little green car and, oh, that car was hot. The seats were scorching because they were leather and the seatbelts were deadly: if one touched your thigh, goodbye to you. With all of us crammed in there and Travis with his leg thrown up on the dashboard plotting our next move, we looked a little like Washington crossing the Delaware. Owen, for his part, stood on the bumper with one egg in each hand like the world's saddest hood ornament or maybe Lady Justice.

What you might be wondering is whether Frankie and

the Mechanic were in love with each other, and while I can't speak for the Mechanic, I can say for sure that they were not. Frankie was not made of sterner stuff necessarily, but she was, as I said, a terrific snob and every snob has her limits.

Even in the open air Frankie's car smelled like dogs, like someone's dog had imbued the leather seats with its essence. Behind the gear shift there was a set of keys and a scrunchie for Frankie's yellow hair and a cassette tape of Patsy Cline called 'Death Cannot Kill What Never Dies', or something like that, and another by Richard Wagner. The cassette by Richard Wagner had a picture of what looked like two extremely white ladies suspended on wires, clutching each other's heads in an almost tender way, and the ladies were made of marble so actually they were statues and it must have taken for ever to chisel in all those little tendrils of hair, and while you could respect the effort, you would really have to wonder who has the time. The ladies were lovely, though, like aerated cream, and you could be sure that they thought well of each other if no one else. Abi was nowhere to be seen.

'What should we do?' one of us asked.

And because it was framed as a question, which implied the possibility of many kinds of answers, no one said 'Let's get a grownup' for fear, maybe, of being too obvious.

'Owen, get down from there,' Autumn barked at Owen, who was now standing on the hood of the car, the very spot, in fact, where the Mechanic had first revealed the notion of constellations, because actually

Owen was looking very unsteady on his spindle legs, but Owen shook his head *no* and pointed left, and though his face was always a tiny stretched canvas of fear and pain, it was doubly so now. We looked left despite our best intentions and here is what we saw:

From the precarious safety of Frankie's car we could see her shed in the foreground, with its impenetrably small windows and buoys tied to its face like it needed help staying afloat in the currents of Frankie's blue-gravel drive, which petered out into an *alien shore* of pine needles and fern and blackberry bushes and pine trees, scaly and red, and aimed, as it were, straight up at the hot clear sky. And though we couldn't see it, of course we knew our parents' childhood home was back there somewhere and this was all, you might say, so far so good. Yes, yes, so far so good. If our parents had come out at this very moment, they would have said 'Get off Frankie's car' and you couldn't have blamed them at all for not seeing the other thing, for instance, because it was only a thing you could feel, which was *thickness*, like a layer of translucent fat over an otherwise ordinary scene. Or a snail's glutinous mantle.

We stared and the thickness wobbled a little as a bird burst from the pine boughs, so we knew that there were living things in there, that the scene was very much alive and well, and then the thickness set again and Autumn said, 'What is it?', which was an invitation to silence.

'Abi?' Travis called out, like olly olly oxen free.

Abi's name arced over our heads and was absorbed into the thickness, or else just slid off, but either way it didn't make it. The glutinous mantle sat still and waited, and us too, but not in the same way.

We weren't thinking about constellations at that very moment, it didn't even cross our minds, but that's the absolute power of narrative convention for you. Years have passed and so I'll just insert this bit:

Because farmers and shepherds were the main people hanging around outside at night, they were also the main reporters-back on constellations, and so it was a fairly humble pursuit which appealed enormously to us, glued as we were to the circumstances of our age and station. The word 'constellation' means *system of stars* in Greek but it's not a Greek invention, no way, but Mesopotamian, and then older and more diffuse than that – the Mayans, the Egyptians – the stars didn't begin and end with the Greeks. Moreover, carbon dating the idea of constellations depends on whether you believe constellations are just a way of organising the night sky or have some inherent juice of their own, withering crops and anointing all-sorts. And if you believe in the autonomy of stars, then constellations are as old as the absolute eldest star, which is 16 billion years, give or take; older than our ability to observe them, three and a half times older than the Earth. In the latter case, then, you would need to believe that, without anything human for the stars to interact with, an object's *capacity* for action is the same as action itself, which is investing a lot of faith in the power of potential. I could go on, I really could, but my main point is that what the Mechanic showed us was the celestial machine above our heads.

Please consider this an intermission.

6. Intermezzo: A Day Out

Here's a story about Frankie: One summer Frankie took some of us kids hiking in the White Mountains. The idea was that Frankie would borrow one of the uncles' station wagons and be back in time for dinner, easy peasy. Someone even took their family dog, who was small and the colour of an apricot and therefore entirely unsuited to the project. Frankie wore cut-offs and a tank top, which showed her brown, ape-strong arms, and her yellow hair was piled on her head like suds, all of which made us realise that she was, in fact, very beautiful. She had little, light-coloured eyes like grape seeds and a nose which she referred to as 'ski-jump'. She was very happy that we had been entrusted to her and her happiness made us happy as well. We were all incredibly happy.

It was, I believe, a small mountain, but of course it was megalithic to us, who were much smaller than even its smallest mappable feature. It was hard-going at first and there was a fair whack of complaining, but the woods smelled so nice and the path was so perfectly made for our little legs – a *challenge*, Frankie told us – that after a while we fell into a rhythm and just watched the back of the person in front of us and learned things about the ropes and pulleys of our legs and knees and swatted at mosquitoes, finding satisfaction in really blasting the ones who were already like blood-filled balloons. And the thing is that when you walk like this, every rock is a mountain, or the mountain becomes its rocks, and you break down a little as well, becoming your constituent parts which doesn't include your mind, and you can suddenly imagine living your life as an ancient farmer or some other purely physical being with no finer thoughts whatsoever except for, I guess, the stars.

When we reached the top of the mountain, we were really gross but we felt good, we felt tired in a long-haul sort of way rather than the short bursts of incredible energy we normally expended, which were often broken up by long periods of torpor. Even the dog seemed pleased with itself. The world, as we saw it then, was a shallow but infinite basin of rippling green with no one in it but us. It was marvellous. We sat down and crossed our legs and looked up at Frankie, who had her arms wide open in a way that can only be described as ecstatic.

'Oh, kids, oh, kids,' she said, and it was in this moment of communal exaltation that we realised she wasn't wearing a backpack.

'I'm hungry,' someone said.

Frankie turned her head with her arms still open as if she were trying to get us to feast on the view, which, of course, we already had.

'Look at this, kids,' she tried again. 'I mean, it doesn't get better than this.'

The cold horror of what she was trying to tell us crested and broke.

'Don't you have any food, Frankie?'

Frankie lowered her arms.

'Didn't you guys have breakfast?'

'Yes,' we said, 'we did.' We suddenly felt that perhaps Frankie wasn't a three-mealer, that maybe the central meal which we called lunch was a relic of childhood – anything was possible – but no, we had seen grownups eating lunch, of course we had. They did it all the time.

'Do you have anything to drink?'

Now, you might wonder at us not noticing before or asking for water or food up till this point, but what we wanted more than anything was to be seen as steely-eyed despite our occasional complaints, so we had held off. We had held off, but now that the dam had been breached it was a real scene. Even the dog got in on it.

'Oh, kids,' Frankie was lamenting, 'it just didn't occur to me that you wouldn't be able to power through.'

One of the smaller ones sobbed. A mid-pack cousin kept saying, 'But I just can't understand.' The dog danced around on its hind legs with its tongue out like a deranged circus performer. It was, all in all, sort of funny, but the humour was lost on us in the moment.

'Well,' Frankie finally sighed, her disappointment hanging off her in wet feathers, 'let's just get back down, then.'

The first few minutes of the descent were as normal as you could hope for under the circumstances: a couple of us really clutching at our stomachs and clicking our dry tongues against the roofs of our mouths to illustrate our predicament, another opting to stagger around instead. Frankie had the littlest one on her shoulders, who in those days was not Abi but Owen; Abi was only just born and even Frankie knew not to take a baby up a mountain. It was not great but it was fine.

And then, from nowhere, the air just kind of lifted like opening a fridge door and the sky grew a peevish cast and it started to rain, fat rain, fat, warm rain, so big it made an actual splat with every drop. Splat. We knew this because we were not under trees like on the way up but on a smooth inverted bowl of stone.

'A little rain never hurt anyone.' Frankie must have been desperate by that juncture and her point was weakly received.

After a few moments, the stone was absolutely glassy. We slipped and slid and Frankie's knees just pooped out and thunder percussed and lightening fizzed and, eventually, Frankie dropped to her butt and took the stone surface like a slide with Owen hunched around her head.

And then it was over.

The rain drew itself shut, it disappeared, it was revoked. The sun crawled out from behind the clouds and everything steamed. Frankie lay on her back in a puddle with her eyes shut, delicately, and Owen released himself from her head and we all stared. Frankie in the sun, depleted, surrounded on all sides by glittering water. She opened one eye and shut it again, and then she laughed. It was a truly fantastic laugh, maybe the best we'd ever heard, like the laugh was not a baby's laugh but an actual baby, something new and bright.

'Hey!' It was a cousin. 'Over here!'

While Frankie lay steaming in her puddle, we picked

blackberries. Blackberries are either delicious or taste like watery cat piss, and because these were the delicious variety we tore them in handfuls and ate until we got bored and then brought some over to Frankie, who opened her mouth and we put one in and then another until we got bored, and then we tried to put one up her nose and then one between her eyes, and we really festooned her and she let us, she was that crapped out, and the berries, I remember, shone.

We loved Frankie, actually. Despite everything, we really did.

Also, you may be wondering where Travis was in the story about the White Mountains. He was there but he hadn't yet achieved his current standing in our hearts, so he was just another cousin then, barely worth mentioning, probably picking at a scab or grappling with his crotch in secret.

Intermission over.

7. Dining Room

No one wanted to get out of the car.

The treeline glistened fatly, more than it had any right to, and we *knew*. It was telling us. It was letting us know.

One of the little ones piped up to say that they weren't feeling so well, but we told them to hush and we listened, because we had no choice. It was the sound of something violent happening underwater, maybe, smothered by an awful weight of soundlessness. Owen's little mouth was opened in the exact shape of one of his eggs. The air was very hot.

'I'm—' Travis was thinking. He put his hand on the back of his neck, which was shaved and had fairly large and painful-looking marks where pimples used to be. 'I'm just going to check it out, but listen. OK, but listen.' He rubbed at his neck like it was very sore indeed. 'It's just me. You guys go back inside. I'll be just a minute, OK, guys?'

Oh, we should not have let him go. Oh, forgive us, but we were so small and he was a giant, he was a vertical cenotaph, golden and perfect. Travis climbed out of the car and the sound of his feet on the gravel made us sick.

We watched him go, Travis, Travis, we watched him lope in his stripes and formal collar towards the trees, the red flag on his scratched leg waving in and out. We

watched him stop at the shoreline where the pine needles pushed up against the gravel and we watched him
rub his neck a second and final time, and then we
watched him disappear.

The mantle wobbled, accepting him, and reset. There
was no sound now. We didn't make a single sound.

How long? How long did the watching go on? Autumn
could have told us for sure, but we didn't ask her. A
while, and then it transformed again into waiting, so I
don't know, is the answer. A very long while.

All during this time we didn't worry about the thing
on the loose in the gravel. For reasons that were both
unclear and also very and keenly defined, we knew that
whatever it was had gone beyond the mantle or created
the mantle in its passing. Everything encased in the
mantle looked both more beautiful and more indistinct
than it would have on just an ordinary day, trapped
behind an excessive amount of high-gloss shellac like
that apple in *Snow White*, or Snow White herself in the
glass coffin, or just the whole sickly enterprise of the
movie, really.

What I'm saying is that the scene presented to us in
that long period of waiting was horribly fixed and at the
same time living, and we had simply let Travis walk into
it and we were filled with dread topped with a scummy
layer of remorse.

'Travis?' we called, and of course there wasn't any
answer. His name just thwacked against the mantle like a
bird against a windowpane. Autumn took a very big
breath while she tried to come up with an executive

command, but in the meantime one or the other of us said, 'Let's get a grownup.'

'OK,' we agreed; it was time.

We descended from the car, with Owen going last, and we helped him down from the hood and then crunched back to the house, which was, after all, only maybe twenty feet or so away, nothing at all. The jockey was there with his lantern, and though he was redundant he was a welcome sight, with his hand in his pocket like he was rooting around for something even better than light to give you, like everything he had was yours for the taking even though he didn't have anything we couldn't see already.

We swung open the screen door and the smell of Frankie's stupid house was terrific, but there was no time for homecoming. Travis was in the trees and someone would need to get him out and we were not up to it so it would have to be a grownup, which meant roping them in on Abi's disappearance, which meant trouble, but we were past that now.

Out on the deck, Aunt Maureen was standing with her back to the house and Frankie was cowering, and they were hip-deep in a verbal ruckus, and the uncles were exhaling or studying their knuckles, and Pin was grim-faced in the corner with her Becks, her hair short like a knight's or something where it used to be long and braided before the divorce, and they all, in one way or another, seemed to be enjoying themselves. Here is what they were talking about:

'God help me, she was just a *textbook* brutalist—'

'That's not what brutalist mea—'

'Oh come off it, OK, *fasc*—'

'Maureen.'

'OK, fine. Beezy was brutal, that's all I'm saying. Frankie, Frankie, hello?'

'I am, I'm listen—'

'I don't want to be harsh. I don't want to be hurtful, but Beezy used you, Frankie, and look, God's honest truth, there's nothing you love more than being use—'

'Maureen, stop—' This was her husband, Uncle Steve, again, who sounded tired.

'No, listen, just listen to what I'm saying for once. She was a snob and a brutalist—'

'Maureen, that's not what br—'

'Beezy was brutal and you liked it and she rewarded you for it and, I mean, look at all this,' Aunt Maureen's arms were out, gesturing to the fiefdom, 'what's all this if no—'

'I just don't know what—' This was Frankie now, who had her head down like Aunt Maureen was beating her about the neck, and though we couldn't see her face, it was clear she was like a cat, purring.

'It's like she won't let you go, for Pete's sake—'

'Mom?' Autumn was at Pin's side, pinging her mom's bra strap. Pin took a battle-weary sip from her bottle of Becks and her eyes were simply locked on the horizon. 'Mom?'

One by one we tried, first with our own parents, and then moving outwards, tugging, whispering, whining, but they were caught. We could see them and they must have seen us, but it was useless. One of the uncles was wearing a t-shirt that said 'To Err is Human, To Forgive Is Not Our Policy', and it had a bib of sweat down the front like what they were doing was very taxing rather than just sitting down. We needled his red arm and he gently swatted us away.

They were transfixed on the bright star of past transgressions and nothing we could do seemed to unfix them:

'How could you be so naive? Come on, fill me in—'

'I—'

'I mean, all I want to know in the world is—'

'That's what she's trying to tell you, Maur—'

No one touched Frankie, though. Frankie couldn't help us because she too busy having fun not helping herself. Her yellow hair had sunshine all through it but the rest of her was in shadow.

'Abi,' we said, 'is gone.'

'And now,' we said, 'Travis is gone too.'

Even Aunt Maureen, whose entire worldly store of children was in jeopardy, was deaf to our entreaties. Her great grey wings were spread. She wasn't crying but her voice sounded like it wanted to, and she rested her hand on one of the smallest one's heads to quieten them down while she spoke.

'Frankie, you brought her, you drove her down there, and what did you think was going to happen?'

'Aunt Maureen,' we said, 'Abi and Travis are gone.'

'I didn't know—'

'Bullshit. And then all this—'

'Maureen.'

'Aunt Maureen, Abi and Travis are gone.'

'I didn't know, I didn't, Maureen, please—'

'They're gone, Aunt Maureen,' our hysteria rising a little, 'we can't find them. Uncle Steve, they're gone.'

Oh, it was absurd, because although we were used to being ignored by adults, we had always assumed that when the day came for immediate action, our words would cut through. A facile kind of ignoring, we'd pegged it as, a thin and friable sort. But now we realised that the wall separating us from our parents was sturdy-as-anything and we couldn't help but feel bad for our past selves, who had been labouring under the misapprehension that they were part and parcel with their families.

We were reaching peak desperation which was going to start involving pinching, when Owen, who had been standing in the frame of the sliding doors, an egg in each hand, took a backwards step into the house and toppled, arms windmilling, onto his skinny butt, and though it was clear that he and his eggs were fine, it was, somehow, enough to make the smallest pause, the tiniest chink, while everyone considered whether he was hurt and decided he wasn't. In this moment, Autumn, who was now our leader, though we would never have called her that, took a breath and shouted, 'Abi's been gone since for almost two hours ago and we can't find her!', to which Aunt Maureen responded with a rapid, multi-part blink, like someone experiencing sunlight for the first time, and then replied, 'No, she's not. She was just here.'

We looked around. The strangeness of the day had made it perfectly plausible that we would simply see Abi now, back amongst us, her tiny teeth packed with orange Cheez Ball dust, and we experienced the twin feelings of relief and disappointment that accompany the end of a crisis, but actually she wasn't.

'Aunt Maureen, hey, Aunt Maureen, where did she go?'

Aunt Maureen was keen to finish her thought and had filled her lungs with sustaining air, which she let out now in an anticlimactic hiss.

'Oh, I don't know, outside? Why don't you kids go look for her?'

'We have, we are, but she's gone.' Autumn's tiny brain was floundering.

'No, she's not, she was just here.' And with that Aunt Maureen, regal in her loose linen jumpsuit and with her long, ash-coloured hair, dismissed us as all the grownups manned their crank shafts and winch hooks and started up the great machine again.

Back in the dining room, we paused to reflect. We were two down and alone at sea.

Next to each of the plates on Frankie's dining table was a white cloth napkin that had been folded in four and then rolled so its corner stuck out unpleasantly like a tongue. In the centre of the table was what Frankie referred to as her *majolica*, which we assumed was a fancy word for bowl but wasn't. Frankie's majolica was huge, the size of Owen's torso, and from a distance looked like a rowboat on its wedding day, but when you got closer you realised that it was pictures of children and men.

The children were kneeling on what looked like lettuces, their heads bowed under a garland's weight. The men, on the other hand, were just wicked faces with horns that were smooth extensions of their foreheads, and also they weren't doing any of the work. They were, essentially, creeps.

We didn't like Frankie's majolica but at the same time it held a great fascination for us because it was *wrong*. It was not the kind of thing you should put food into, though we could imagine, somehow, food coming out of it: meat on splintery bones and strange, jewelled fruit covered in pesticide, that sort of thing. Stuff that would call to you and then make you very sick indeed. It's possible we thought this because Frankie had told us her majolica was *glazed with lead* and, if you can remember, it was high season for lead poisoning that summer; everyone convinced it was in the walls, in the air, that we were all just inferior versions of our rightful selves, bumping around, understanding less than ever before.

As we reflected, we found ourselves fanning out around the table and each taking a seat in one of Frankie's insane, high-backed chairs. Owen placed an egg to either side of his plate but not on his plate: that would have been both an invitation and an obscenity. Autumn sat at one end of the table, and the other end was, of course, empty. Besides the spot where Travis should have been, all the chairs were full. We only thought about that later, though. We weren't at that point yet, where every last thing was bristling with poignancy.

Autumn cleared her throat but had nothing to say. It

must have been hard for her especially, I suppose, because she had managed to lose her two benefactors, the two children on whom she and her brother depended for their charity and fellow-feeling every afternoon over the summer break while Pin sorted herself out. It was unclear how things were going with that. Autumn wanted us all to believe that it was going great, but it wouldn't be nice, would it, to be a guest in someone's house for most of your day, with no bed to lie down on if you were sleepy, for instance, with snacks that were not your own and a father who was not your own. But then there was Travis, and even though he would have probably ignored you most of the time, even though he would be off practising his French horn or learning C++ or whatever, he would still have to pay you some attention some of the time and that, I think, would almost make it worth it.

Two years later, a movie would come out called *Hook* that we all really liked but apparently was critically panned, though none of us read the reviews because children don't. If you haven't seen it, *Hook* is about Peter Pan, who has grown up into a lawyer and fattened grotesquely and forgotten all his magic and his whole life, in fact, but Captain Hook hasn't! Oh, no, Captain Hook tracks Peter Pan down to Wendy's house in London and kidnaps Peter Pan's kids, who think their dad is a rigid, absent bore, and Peter Pan has to go with Julia Roberts to Neverneverland to get them back. It's a great movie.

Anyway, because Peter Pan is out of shape and unrecognisable as Peter Pan, he has to do lots of physical and mental exercises to regain his place as the head of the Lost Boys, displacing Rufio, the beautiful and tragic leader who doesn't have any faith in grownups at all but more or less sacrifices himself for Peter, who has won his respect by flying around shouting insults at people.

In an earlyish scene, Peter Pan sits down to eat with the Lost Boys and there's nothing on the table and Peter Pan is starving from all his exercising and everyone else is licking their lips in an over-the-top way and then they dig in, really relishing every mouthful. It's very touching, actually, how happy all the boys are sharing their food and all you can see is empty silver cloches pouring steam and these boys passing invisible things along to each other like a real family, which is what they all long for. It's a metaphor, probably, for the shackles of belief being a stronger bond than empirical evidence, but Peter Pan is just blind to it all because he doesn't need it like they do.

Anyway, it all comes to a head when Peter Pan flings an invisible spoonful of something at Rufio and the table is suddenly alight with food: it's an act of joyful violence that gains entry for Peter Pan to this imaginary family, and that seems about right, but here's the second and most horrifying thing: *this is not food that kids would eat.* It is absolutely and 100 per cent the kind of food that would come out of Frankie's majolica, jutting heaps of shiny, underdone chicken and dates and cream pies the inedible colours of original playdough, everything in heavy pewter dishes. It is truly awful. At first I thought it was a misstep on the creator's part, but now I think it was a deliberate commentary on the warping effects of alienation on children.

Steven Spielberg has said that he's slightly ashamed of *Hook*, but I really can't see why: Dustin Hoffman is a revelation. You should see it if you haven't already; you could watch it at any time if you wanted.

This is a very long-winded way of saying that Autumn had failed us.

Autumn had failed us and was now presiding over an empty table opposite the ghost of her more admired predecessor. It must have felt bad but we didn't care. Her dark hair fell around her shoulders and though it was very beautiful in that moment, the face peering out of it was not. It was despondent and out of options. She hmmm'ed a little and drummed her fingers and pretended to look around the room for inspiration. The hopelessness of the afternoon crept like sunlight over the table and filled our plates and then someone suggested watching TV, and though that person didn't turn to a pile of ashes in their seat they should have.

You could see the appeal shivering along the ranks.

There was an audacious scraping of chairs as we prepared ourselves to drift – how easy it would have been. But in this general loosening there were two holdouts sitting at their place settings, drawing us back from our own feeble desires. It was Autumn and Owen.

Over the years, one of the things that has plagued me most is the question of who made the decision to stay, and who stayed to support the other, because actually I think it might be braver to do something foolish powered only by someone else's conviction than acting on any conviction of your own. I don't know. What I do remember is Autumn sitting there, gripping the sides of her chair, and Owen with an egg in each hand, and so, for the shame of it all, we stayed, the promise of TV fading like a dying star but more quickly.

'OK,' said Autumn, checking her watch and then looking at Owen, who nodded, 'I think probably we should go back outside.' And like the battle-weary soldiers we always thought we wanted to be, we turned back towards the door, our admiral at the helm, the eggs' tiny mother hewing close behind.

8. Intermezzo: The Lilac Swing

One theory is that Beezy felt that her children should have been unhappy but brilliant. That she would have liked, ideally, to see pictures of them under dust jackets, with cigarettes and expressions that were frank or cool or melancholic or wry, summering in some rocky and expensive cove. Wool sweaters rather than wool-mix, coils of rope and boxes of specialty bond ordered in from *Newyaak* and then collected at the general store post counter in boat shoes, that kind of thing. *Yass, Baabra, the maanuscript will be with ya baa Saadaday.* That is to say she wanted for them to be loved by the world collectively, if not so much by the world's constituent members, but when they started doing pedestrian things like choosing high-school Spanish over French and showing interest in car magazines, she just threw in their towel.

The fact is that Beezy wanted to be a writer herself, which we knew because she wrote a novel called *The Lilac Swing*. She got Frankie to type it up and she even had it bound.

The heroine of Beezy's book, from what I've read, is a young woman named Evelyn Southall, who packs for long weekends down the Cape and can often be found checking in with her answering service. Evelyn has a best friend named Doreen, whose body is always threatening to erupt from her clothes and sighs things rather than says them. Evelyn's body, on the other hand, is nicely contained and she likes to take her gloves off and place them in her handbag and also to 'snap her handbag shut'. Everyone drinks dry sherry.

Frankie and Beezy had worked on it while Frankie was caring for Beezy. It was part of the service, probably. Beezy dictated it to Frankie, who had just finished secretarial school, and Frankie typed it up and then gave it to Beezy to read over, and then Beezy dictated the corrections, and they did this again and again until the manuscript was perfect and there was no trace of Frankie left in it.

'We didn't see them for months,' our parents told us, 'Frankie must have lost twenty pounds.'

I suppose expectations were high because Beezy had been a sensational storyteller was the thing, though none of our parents could remember her stories, or else they just wanted to keep them for themselves. When we thought of Beezy telling stories, all we could picture was her face moving with the sound off, her eyes going wide with surprise and her hands moving in and out, spinning and stretching a bright, ectoplasmic skein between them. I think what she was doing was practising and her family, in her mind, were her first audience but not her best. Though ultimately they were both first and best because they were her only, but she wouldn't have known that then.

'Did Beezy ever get it made into a real book?' And

our parents shook their heads and, although they didn't say why, it was clear to us that they thought the book was no good. You could tell from the way they looked surprised at their own embarrassment, like they hadn't expected to be so touched by Beezy's vulnerability, but now that they'd remembered it was too awful, like seeing a bruise on the back of someone's heel.

Anyway, I never read past the first few pages of *The Lilac Swing* and so I'm afraid to say that I don't know what the lilac swing was, but it would have been a symbol of one kind or another.

9. Road

It was not nice to be back outside. Some of us hung around at the doorway, hoping to be recalled. A couple of us inspected the jockey while others sat down and stood up and then sat back down again. The jockey seemed really pleased now that we were paying him attention, like it was all he lived for. He mingled, the ingratiating shrimp, and so we dropped down onto our haunches and really gave him the once-over, and we saw for the first time what our parents meant when they said *get rid of it.*

'Come on,' Autumn said.

Over the gravel we went, past the safety of the cars. What would have been really good at that moment would be to have seen Travis parting the mantle with Abi in a fireman's carry. We would have even settled for bupkis, for nothing, for a resumption of watching and waiting, because we knew how to do that. But what we got, as we drew closer, was the unctuous, flippered feeling that nothing had changed in a really horrible way, that what was lying behind the mantle, the varnished scene, was only *pretending* to be the same as before for reasons of its own. I suppose we could have felt reassured that the forest wasn't as clever as it thought, but a wolf in a lousy costume is still a wolf. A bird burst from the pine boughs and the scene wobbled like it was following a stage direction. The air was swollen with midday heat.

We stood at the perimeter, our sneakers nosed up against the last railroad tie. With the exception of Owen, our arms hung nearly down to our knees, like we were holding suitcases and watching a puff of steam move towards us through trees.

Who was the first in line through? Would you believe me if I said I can't remember?

It's true, though, it may have been Autumn.

I think it probably was.

Autumn was the first one through and we all filed in behind her. You could see it up close, like wet rubber cement, separating the woods from the house, but unlike rubber cement it had no smell and as we passed through it we felt nothing, not even a shiver, but we still knew, every last one of us, that we had emerged into an entirely different place with probably different rules. When we looked back, the gelatinous layer had been transposed onto the gravel drive, the cars, the jockey, Frankie's house and everything beyond, and it felt awfully sad, like really saying goodbye, whereas normally the sadness only comes later.

Oh, in a way it was beautiful in there, all the different qualities of light in one space: the shadows cast by our bodies, the spangled green-yellow-violet display of the blackberry bushes, the warm red sunspots on the forest floor, the brilliant jets of blue between the needle tips of the pines. Forests are really just a repetition of patterns.

It's why people lose their minds in forests and also on oceans: the human brain needs disruption, I think, and that's why we make things. You could say that an artist, for instance, finds patterns in everything, but I think probably what an artist is really there to do is to tear a big hole in the maddening patterns, to create something that is so itself that it repels everything around it. I'm all for artificiality, is what I'm saying. It's what humans bring to the table.

'Travis?' we tried calling. 'Abi? Travis?'

It was quiet and close and it would have made a very satisfying diorama, though making all of us would use up a lot of clay, so maybe you would need just to focus on the big names at a key moment.

'Travis? Abi?'

It's hard to sculpt someone calling out. It just looks like they're burping. And that's probably what it felt closest to in there, the feeling of trying to say something while a burp travels outwards, your inner gases fighting with your deepest yearnings. We were, it has to be said, very scared.

We were scared because it's a bad feeling to look for one thing when it is equally likely you'll find the very thing you've been avoiding – in our case, the zipping thing and whatever friends it might have – when your odds are 50/50. Besides a certain level of jumpiness, your motivations become complicated. We started looking behind trees like we'd forgotten that we weren't really playing hide and seek, and once we started we couldn't stop. Some of us nudged small rocks over with the toe of a sneaker. Others cleared pine needles away so we could get a clear view of the dirt. Our actions had stopped making any sense, actually, but the less sense they made the more we felt compelled to do them: to search under smaller and smaller objects – a leaf, an errant bit of blackberry cane. We checked over each other's work, turning stones that had already been turned, etc. It was a feeling that many of us would return to later with the advent of the internet and it would have been very frustrating to watch, I imagine, so it's probably quite frustrating to read, and for that I can only apologise. I can't explain it further than to say that it happened and that it would have gone on indefinitely, as Abi and Travis spun further and further away from us into the void, if the forest hadn't made its first real mistake. The forest got cocky, was what happened: it was so tickled watching us waste our time that it sent a bird bursting in from the direction of the driveway as a provocation, but here's the thing: birds *never* burst *into* trees, only ever *out* of them, but this forest didn't know that! It wasn't equipped with that very basic fact. The absolute oddity of a bird materialising from a clear, open sky in a clamour of feathers and, with the same velocity, hurtling pell-mell into a tree stopped us in our tracks.

'Uh, I don't think they're here,' is what someone said, and someone else replied, 'No, I don't think so,' and you could feel the trees, the ferns, the whole scene just wilt a little with disappointment, and we were disappointed too, of course, though not in the same way, and also a little embarrassed for ourselves.

We took stock. It didn't take long, as all there was was the short corridor of woods we'd combed through and then, in front of us, a long coiling wall of underripe blackberries disappearing into the trees in both directions. The childhood home was just beyond this wall; we couldn't see it but we knew it had to be there. It was the only logical place to go, we supposed.

'OK, guys, follow me!' Autumn had clearly been giving herself a pep talk because she marched up to the wall of blackberry bushes and reached both arms in and tried to part it like she was Moses, but unlike Moses she had no one looking out for her so she just snagged her watchband on the coils and got really scratched up.

'Oooh,' Autumn said, rubbing her arms. We looked down the wall, which sloped gently into the forest proper, and then in the other direction, which at worst went on until it reached the road, which couldn't be more than a few minutes at most, so that's the way we went. Although it wasn't anything special, just a road with the occasional meadow running alongside it or a mailbox set on a post at the end of a drive that promised the existence of a house you never saw, we thought about it with warmth. So few cars passed this way that they hardly ever repaired it and it was eaten away by winter after winter of neglect, which was how the residents who'd buried themselves deep in the woods on either side preferred it, I think – to be inaccessible to those without chutzpah and/or soft suspensions. We walked towards the road along the wall of inedible blackberries.

'What time is it, Autumn?' we asked, but she just looked at her watch and gave a thoughtful 'mmm', which was meant to convey the impression of an admiral scrutinising nautical charts and annoyed us to no end.

We hadn't needed to ask because, really, we knew: it was lunchtime. Past lunchtime, even. We walked and the green-faced berries just bubbled off their stems unappealingly. Without warning, one of the littler ones ignored everything that nature was trying to tell them and reached out and twisted a berry right off the wall and shoved it in their mouth, their face curdling to the point where it looked just like the thing they'd tried to ingest and they said 'pah'. *Oh*, we thought, *we wish you had not done that*, because of course it led to the following:

'I'm hungry,' someone said, and suddenly we all were, now that we were on the move and our fear of the zipping thing had dissipated somewhat, 'does anyone have anything to eat?'

We all shook our heads to indicate that we had absolutely nothing to eat. Probably the adults would be starting up the grill at this point, probably there were bowls of tortilla chips making the rounds. If we were where we were meant to be, we would be stuffed by this point, beautifully sick with food, and we thought about all this with not a little regret as we walked. We imagined the adults having set aside their differences, breaking bread together, which in this case was hot dogs and chicken skewers and fruit salad with watermelon balls. Would they be wondering where we were?

If we looked deep in our hearts, we knew they

probably would be grateful mostly for our absence. It was enough to make us weep, and that's when we realised that we were too hungry to do any of this correctly. We were getting agitated.

'Autumn?'

Autumn was at the head of the line and she pretended not to hear. Her long hair swung against her back and what it looked like to us was a flapping tarpaulin on the back of a farm truck which was disappearing from view.

'Autumn?'

If anything, she sped up. She was trying to outrun our demands but we weren't having it. Her plump, scratched-up arms. You have to understand that despite the better angels of our nature, a body needed food.

'Autumn, what time is it? We're hungry!'

We could see Frankie's house behind us through the trees: it was close enough to see the awful whites of the jockey's eyes, but gelatinated. This was all turning out to be an utter disaster, what absolute carnage – first Frankie's ominous majolica, now a cornucopia of underripe berries. With tears in our eyes, we thought of that day in the White Mountains when everything was sweet and good and lucky, but that day was not this one. Looking back, we should have taken it as a sign.

'Autumn!'

Autumn was hurrying, hurrying, her busy self striving towards the road, and we were following, but more like chasing, suddenly, and we were nearing the road now, we could see its sinuous curve through the breaks in the trees, but we were consumed and it was a promise that no longer mattered. It wasn't there, this hunger, and then it was.

'Auuuutumn! Auuuutumn!' we bayed – yes, I'm ashamed to say, that was the word for it – hot on her heels, and what we were demanding from her was a feeding.

'Auuuutuuuuuuuuuuuuuumn!'

Anything could have happened in the moment right before we reached the road. Who knows what we would have done, what we were capable of, who knows, but then Autumn stopped on a dime and said, 'Look—' her voice a mixture of wonder and relief, 'oh my gosh, look at that!'

We looked down at the road, wet-mouthed, and we saw – scattered down the centre of this road, right down the yellow line, was a trail of Oh Henry!s flattened to the thickness of a pencil by passing cars but otherwise unviolated.

Stop! you're probably shouting; however I relate all this in the full understanding of what it means to be a child presented with miraculous candy in the woods, even when it's squashed. If it had been one shining Oh Henry! sat on a toadstool in a beam of damp sunlight, we wouldn't have gone near it. But we were suddenly on the border of civilisation, you see, and there were so many Oh Henry!s meandering down the road into the distance that they could only have come off a vending machine delivery van, a busted box and an open door – it must have been that. It seemed to us, starving as we were, both accidental and providential, a fantastical mixture of both, and we slid down the embankment and ran along the road, scooping them up and shoving them in our pockets and crying 'I got one!' each and every time, those sunny yellow bars.

If you don't know what an Oh Henry! is, I pity you, because they are delicious and also now defunct, I believe. They don't loom large on the cultural landscape but they are chocolate and nuts and fudge and caramel and hence keep their shape more or less when pressed into the earth by 3,000 pounds of steel. We deposited them into a common store and then ran back for more: there must have been at least a hundred of them in the distance. Some of us started chasing the trail over the hill, some of us were sitting right in the middle of the road admiring the abundance, when someone shouted 'Car!' and the cry was carried along from child to child, 'Car! Car!', and we skittered back to the shoulder and waited and we could hear the warm tremor of an oncoming vehicle. We could feel it like thunder rolling across a valley, but unlike thunder nothing followed, no sparkling release of electricity. The road stayed empty except for our feast.

It was strange, all of us sitting back against the embankment, listening hard for nothing at all, and we looked at the remaining bars and realised that we would trade them for a passing car, actually, a station wagon with a 'My Child Made the Honour Roll' bumper sticker and some stupid kids looking back at us, on their way to somewhere entirely pedestrian like the laundromat. Maybe it would have been someone we knew, even. They could have slowed and rolled down the window and said, 'Hey, what are you kids up to?' and then we would have said, 'Oh, you know,' and then we could have asked them how their summer was going and vice versa. That would have been good.

We sat down, drew up our knees, and ate. Only Owen wasn't partaking, so we peeled a candy bar for him and fed him in elegant bites while he held his eggs and, in a way, the candy bar was more delicious just watching Owen take these bites than when we took our own, I don't know why. It was, looking back on it, a lovely meal but not the raucous saccharine orgy we had originally envisioned. It was something to do with the car not appearing when it should have, I believe, and I believe that it was probably our first adult meal, consuming something delicious against a backdrop of foreboding. That and the fact that we ate what we could, stuffed some into our pockets, and left the rest behind in a heap. We were getting tired of miracles, though we didn't know it yet.

10. Childhood Home

We crested the little hill at the foot of the drive and there it was. We saw it as if for the first time, although of course it had been a dim presence in the background of photos and behind the trees as our parents' cars slowed up Frankie's drive. We hadn't known about it being a house of great significance, though, until the previous Thanksgiving.

It was post-slap, after dinner but before board games. We'd found Frankie sitting by herself in the empty kitchen with her mouth open and her eyes unfocused but shiny bright. In front of her, surrounded by stacks of dirty plates, was the mince pie no one had eaten, with a weighted cloth over it to keep it as fresh as it was ever going to be.

'Frankie?' We shook her a little. 'Hi, Frankie, do you want to see our show?'

Frankie swam up suddenly from inside herself.

'Oh, you kids,' she said, in a soggy, muffled sort of way. We couldn't see any marks on her face. Her arms dangled on either side of her chair. 'I hope you know how *special* you are.'

We nodded. Our parents and the TV told us on the regular.

Frankie pushed on, half-talking, it seemed, to herself.

'*She* would have thought you were something special, she would have been *besotted.*' There was a smell coming off Frankie or maybe the mince pie, I remember that. 'Me and your moms and dads, we were a real *gang* once upon a time, a get-along gang! Loosey-goosey, a real kick, just in for supper and then back out, we lived,' and like someone had opened a door to a cold room, the condensation had evaporated from her eyes, 'in the house next door, did you know? Oh, didn't you know? What a hoot!' And then her arms lifted and opened to embrace as many of us as she could and, despite ourselves and the smell, we crowded in. 'We were born in that house,' she spoke into our hair. 'Oh, kids, it was marvellous, what marvellous fun we all had.'

Our parents' childhood home.

Now, we looked up the long drive. It was a split-level ranch-type deal with clapboard, and asphalt shingle, and it all looked pretty standard, if you want the honest truth, just like any other house. There were some tiger lilies and forsythia under the windows and a small tree in the front yard to the right of the little porch steps, the kind with yellow cherries you can't eat and exotic-looking palm-ish leaves. Perhaps there had been changes since our parents had lived there, some basic maintenance like keeping the paintwork fresh, a different doormat and curtains etc. There would have had to have been, and though those small details would have been extremely piquant for our parents who could have told you what curtains and doormat should have been there, to us it meant nothing.

Luckily there weren't any cars in the driveway, so we

could assume that no one was home, and it was only while experiencing the relief of this that we realised we had been nervous about what we were going to say if these people came out of their house and asked us what we were doing on their property. Some don't care if you go parading through their yard but others care very much.

'What now?'

We sat down on the grass next to the wall of bracken and the corridor of trees that now separated us from Frankie's house and our parents, who were probably lost in their delirium of memories and grilled meat. We looked at our parents' childhood home, which was dark inside, and tried to imagine them living there.

The movie *Amélie* came out when we were much older, most of us in high school, and even then we didn't watch it till college or later because, though it was French, it was also somehow uncool, too whimsical and over-charming. Anyway, in it the protagonist, Amélie, finds a tin box of childhood memorabilia in her wall, and though it just looks like a bunch of old shit, the extreme care with which it was curated and then hidden makes it clear it was precious to some person of the past and hence to Amélie, who needs, the film posits, to get a life. Adults watching this scene are often very moved. It brings back to them, I think, a time when the smallest things take on a significance that even the largest things later on down the line can't match. To a child watching this film, however, I imagine there is just the ball-ache of being found out – it was such an excellent hiding place and such bad luck that Princess Diana had to go ahead and die at that very moment, and children love to hide things because they're given no sanctuary.

The reason I bring up *Amélie* is that it would have been good to have found that sort of box at the childhood home, maybe nestled in a tree or something, because there was no way we were going inside. It wouldn't have addressed our most pressing concern, the location of Abi and Travis, but it would have shed light on a more clandestine set of questions, which was what our parents had been like when they were our age. We knew, of course, the overall shape of our parents' childhood because it was most of what they talked about at family functions: the family forgetting Pin at home on a trip to the beach, and when they came back Pin had been bitten by a racoon. An able-bodied Beezy taking the kids on a sailing trip and then staying in a hotel while the kids slept on the boat. Stories of preventable accidents and general hurt feelings on a micro level, and strokes and divorces on the macro, whereas there must have been a lot of other stuff that filled up their days, which is the actual material of childhood – a really one-of-a-kind bouncy ball, for instance, or a whorl in a piece of driftwood that had become a face as familiar to them as those of their siblings – the reminder of which unmanned Amélie and, later, us.

'Maybe they went in the house? Maybe we should knock?' a little one suggested.

We squatted with our backs to the offal of greenery and looked at the house. Autumn checked her watch for no reason.

'You do it, then.'

'I thought of it so you do it.'

'You do it.'

'Guys!'

Autumn stood up.

'Um . . .' You could tell that she'd stood up with real purpose and was now regretting it. We looked at her and, for the first time, thought that maybe she was getting a little fat. She looked nothing like Pin, whose real name was Patricia and who was built like a skewer. She looked like Carl, who was good-looking but squishy at the edges. He'd had black hair too, though nothing as glorious as Autumn's. Owen, on the other hand, looked like Pin. Maybe that's how they should divide the kids up. You had to go live with the parent you were most like, but in this case Carl didn't want either, so it wouldn't have worked. In this case, Pin was stuck with both. Autumn pressed a button on her watch, producing a sharp little beep, which she clearly hadn't anticipated because she flinched.

'Right,' she said, to no one in particular, 'it's two o'clock.'

There was a pause. It was the time school normally finished. That was weird to think about.

'Are you going or what, Autumn?' And Autumn looked over her shoulder and nodded like it was a philosophical question.

'Thanks, Autumn,' we said, to seal the deal: gee, thanks, thanks.

Autumn shrugged and, without looking at us, took a

little breath and set off across the lawn. Owen stood, too, with his eggs, but was frozen with indecision, unsure of where his loyalties should lie, with his sister or his babies. Because he was a new mother, he was having to work all this stuff out for the first time. His eyes followed her across the grass and up the little steps, which she took in a jaunty two-at-a-time – credit where credit is due.

'Don't worry, Owen,' we told him. 'She's just going to see, she's just going to knock, don't worry.'

Autumn stood before the door and raised her fist and then froze and turned her head to look at us, who had scooted as far backwards into the blackberry bushes as our pain thresholds would allow. She mouthed something unintelligible, and what we did was give her a big thumbs up, and she mouthed it again and we just shrugged and she turned back to the door, twisted the knob, and walked in.

'Oh no!'

'Oh no, she's gone in!'

It was insane, it was entirely without precedent! She hadn't understood the brief!

'Autumn's gone in the house!'

Squatting on our haunches, we quietly lost our minds, and that's when we heard the sound we'd heard before on the road, only this time it was arriving, it had arrived, it was here, the very definite crunch of gravel under tyres, and what was dismaying about the sound was how comfortable it was, how at home and unawares, that sound.

The owners were back.

A Peep-yellow station wagon came over the hill and rolled to a stop about school-gym-length away from where we were kind of hiding, and we went absolutely still as many possibilities presented themselves, every last one untenable: we could confess or make a break for it or create a diversion. But any of these would take a certain degree of derring-do, so instead we just waited, netted in our own panic.

We heard the car door open and out stepped a lady with shopping bags.

The lady didn't know! She didn't know we were in her house! We examined this lady with mounting fear. She had shorts on and a blouse and tennis shoes with no socks and looked around our parents' age – only this lady was African American! She was African American and she pointed her clicker at her car and the lights flashed and she adjusted the paper bags in her arms and we prayed they would break open all over her yard and she would have to take her time clearing it all up so Autumn could nip out a window. Or else a man could appear with a giant cheque and confetti, and while everyone was celebrating we would make our escape. We watched her walk up the drive. This lady had short hair like Pin's, but unlike our aunt she was wearing lipstick and had glasses, which swung against her chest as she searched around for her house key while trying not to drop everything. She didn't know the door was unlocked! She didn't know!

The woman put the grocery bags down in front of

the door and went back to the car to look for her house keys, presumably, and we hoped Autumn might take this chance to burst from the house like a bird from the mantle but she didn't. Autumn was Goldilocksing it up in there – it was so typical. Owen was breathing tiny fast breaths, one for each very rapid heartbeat.

So the woman was fishing around inside her car and the suspense was really something. Her car had one bumper sticker for Brattle Bookshop and one for Woodman's Clams and one that said 'Join the Rainbow Coalition Vote Mel King for Mayor', but it looked like it had been there for a while, which made us wonder with one part of our constricting minds who Mel King was and whether he'd achieved his dream of being mayor. The Rainbow Coalition sounded not bad, actually; it sounded like something we could have, on a better day, maybe come around to, depending on what they were offering us.

And then she straightened, walked back to the house and up the steps, scooped her bags back into her arms, and opened the door. There was a moment when the key wasn't doing what she thought it should do, when she realised, essentially, that her door was in fact unlocked, and even from our distance we could see a question swim across her face as she went in. She went in! Oh my God.

Even considering the spate of disappearances and the zipping thing and the frenzied animals and the glutinous mantle, this was, up to this point, far and away the most chilling thing that had happened to us all day because we would be forced to explain something ludicrous to an angry stranger. Or Autumn would, at any rate. Maybe we would be gone by that point. Probably we would be out of there.

It was terrible to think about nonetheless. Minutes passed, a good handful of godawful wormy little minutes in which we waited and watched, and then Owen stood.

'No!' We yanked his shirt hem. 'Sit down!'

He took a step forward.

'Owen, you numbskull, sit down!'

Honestly, you really had to wonder sometimes.

And it was just then a 'psssst' hurtled past us from behind and we turned, oh so quietly, and there she was! Autumn's head emerged from behind a tree at the back of the backyard and she did a 'come on!' gesture, and the run across the childhood home's backyard was something I wouldn't like to try again, but we made it, yes, we did! We were horribly exposed, like ants passing over a paper plate, but we crossed the backyard in one frantic dash and then we were there, with Autumn, in the thin prelude to the forest, panting and absolutely shitting ourselves.

'How did you get out? Did she see you? Were they in there?'

Autumn was only seven – I think I've already mentioned that – and though that may seem young to you, for us it was just median. The burden we had placed on her was entirely reasonable, we felt.

It took some prodding but eventually this is what we

got out of her: Autumn had seen the opportunity of an opened door and jumped on it. She relayed this with a somewhat dampened sense of pride. The inside of the house had all the regular things in it and she'd been having a poke around, whispering for Travis and Abi, when she'd heard the door open and by then, of course, it was too late: she was at the far end of the living room and a woman walked in and put her grocery bags on the kitchen counter, but here was the thing:

'She didn't see me,' Autumn told us, nervous all of a sudden, not meeting our collective eye. 'She turned on the radio to the news and put stuff in the fridge and that whole time I was just standing by the sofa.'

'What!' we shouted, under our breaths. 'What are you talking about? Weren't you hiding?'

'No,' she said, 'the kitchen and the living room were the same room with big sliding doors to outside. The lights weren't on. I thought maybe if I stood very still—' She looked like she was going to cry.

We shook our heads in disbelief.

'Did you close your eyes?' a little one asked, and Autumn said that she hadn't. She had just watched the woman from the far corner and waited.

'And then she walked out of the room,' Autumn said, 'and I left out the sliding doors.'

Autumn looked really embarrassed, violated even. It couldn't have been a nice experience, to feel invisible in your own home, which it was in a way, if you thought about it. If things had turned out differently, the child-hood home might have passed to us, so in many ways it *was* ours. We patted Autumn on the shoulder and thought about how next time we would choose our emissaries with more care, and then we looked into the woods, which gathered tighter and tighter until it was just warp and weft.

Later, after everything unfolded, we were given more details on what had happened in the house. Autumn spat the details out like beads of phlegm over a long period, days, weeks, so reluctantly that we never knew if there was perhaps more down there, stewing, waiting to be expectorated into the sink of our brains.

Autumn, it turns out, had gotten distracted and hadn't in fact gone any further than the living room. She had just trailed around, mesmerised in the cool, dark stillness of the childhood home, because there were pictures of a family on the wall – not ours, no, but the woman's family, presumably – and while some of the pictures were from now, others were from a long time ago ('You could tell,' she said, 'by their hair and also some of the pictures were black and white'), from when the woman was a child. It seemed wrong to us and we told her so.

Hang those in your own home, we thought, and there was the crux, there was the meat of Autumn's problem, though it was the last thing she gave us, it was the thing she heaved up last of all: what she insisted on was that many of the pictures were taken at the childhood home at the very same time our parents would have been living there.

'No!' We wouldn't believe it.

We thought about Pin, Frankie, Aunt Maureen, the

uncles in their shorts clutching their boxes of memories, fizzing over with one-of-a-kind plans and dreams and staring into the camera, poised, the heroes of the story. And then we thought how little that photo would mean to this woman; she would just draw a blank and turn back to her kids and groceries or think about what she needed to do at her job the next day. Like we hardly existed at all. It was inconceivable.

Autumn stuck to her story, though. She never retracted it.

But, you ask now, was it? Was it actually the childhood home? Were you dummies mucking around in the wrong place?

I don't know: we never found out. After everything happened, it got lost in the shuffle and then time went by and no one wanted to talk about any of it anymore. Everyone felt it was best to move on. And so I say to you that we were both in the right place and, at the same time, not – I can't explain it any other way.

Also, we were not ghosts. I feel I should clear that up right now.

11. Intermezzo: May Queen

The Lilac Swing is a boring book if you're not related to the author, and even then: 'Many days Evelyn was jolly but today her dahlias had given her *heap big* trouble', that sort of thing. Beezy's world, I can only assume, the one she'd grown up in. Though we'd never seen a picture of Beezy's own childhood home, we'd have drawn it Greek Revivalish with lawn croquet, even though Beezy's father hated Greeks.

Anyway, because of Beezy's patrician vibe and the fact that our parents grew up in a very horses-and-beeswax part of an already pretty aristocratic area of the state, you would have thought they were marked for success. You would have thought they couldn't have avoided it! But well into their youth, each of the five really did their utmost to scupper their own chances in life in utterly idiosyncratic ways, which is the usual province of the middle-to-upper-middle-class. We didn't realise this at the time, of course. To us, our parents were doing just fine.

Take Aunt Maureen. Aunt Maureen was known as the family scholar, or she at least got good grades and participated in sports and organised various events, like protests and bake sales. Because of this she went to what I now know was a very good liberal arts college not so far away and graduated with a degree in Classics, and then met Uncle Steve, who played acoustic guitar and that was the end of that. At one family gathering someone referred to Aunt Maureen as a *hausfrau* and she left the room. Even Aunt Maureen's lovely college, which had original framed architect's drawings of itself from, like, 1793 all over its own walls and giant chalkboards just folded itself up, and now it's the Eastern Seaboard headquarters for a national bank. And because there's no one left at the gates, any old person can say they went there, and where, I ask you, does that leave Aunt Maureen?

And then there's Pin. Pin was remote and gale-scoured and, when she was young, she was in and out of hospitals for dark and unspecified reasons, and she now worked at a plant nursery hauling sacks of composting material across concrete floors. And then, of course, you have her divorce and annoying children.

The uncles, for their part, joined the Navy and then dropped out of the Navy. Then they coasted around for a while, writing postcards from insalubrious locations and sleeping on park benches, and now they had jobs doing manual work, which they on occasion tried to unionise with only the most qualified success.

Frankie, as I've already explained, was Frankie.

What I'm trying to get at here is a question that none of us have been able to answer, which is: so? This is a matrix-based problem, you say, the solution to which is adjusting the criteria with which you judge a life. I hear you. I do.

And it's true that the problem was one of expectation and also one of the lowest order: as we grew older we realised there were vast numbers of people whose problems ran in the opposite direction. Theirs weren't issues of too many resources squandered, for instance, or high expectations dashed, but of resources and expectations thrust into the red, essentially, before they were even born. These problems were related if you want to think about it in terms of distribution, which we obviously did not.

Regardless, our parents were good and loving parents, which is something, and most of their exceptionality was in areas that probably only we could appreciate, like patience and kindness and the ability to find humour in depressing situations. This is what's meant by adjusting the criteria with which you judge a life, but if you haven't noticed, that sort of thing is only handy at junctures of great disruption and upset (when a person is dying, say, or commits an act of great heroism after being a prick) and is pretty weak stuff when pitted against a weekday's flinty realities.

So it was a lame sort of problem but nevertheless it was ours, whose sneaker brands were no indication of our breeding, who have read *Gravity's Rainbow* but also felt the sting of the repossessed car, and to varying degrees it really consumed us.

Here's a story: After Beezy had her stroke but before her husband, who was our grandfather but only in a genealogical sense, legged it, she decided she would relearn to play tennis from her wheelchair, so every day after school she had Frankie and Pin lobbing balls at her while she practised her backhand in the living room of our parents' childhood home. The story is always told in terms of physical and emotional turmoil, but if you told it in another way it could be one of triumph. I want to say a story of triumph of the will, but that's been taken. That one is best left alone.

And another: Even though you probably wouldn't have called her beautiful, Beezy was May Queen her final year of college and she rode at the front of a college parade and waved her wrist at people. You wouldn't have called her beautiful but maybe *handsome*, in that sort of back-handed way people had. You're a HANDSOME woman! No one would like that. It's what you would only ever write about someone after they were dead. Anyway, Beezy was May Queen and we've actually seen a newspaper clipping of her with a bushel of white flowers on her head and a white full-skirted dress and little white gloves to protect her white waving hands and the whole lot. It was a carnival of white. She had a stubborn and maybe prideful demeanour, which is now referred to as resting bitch face. It was, I think, the year before she got married, so she was a free agent and everything in the world was in front of her – no kids, no husband, no nothing.

The caption reads: 'Then with merry shouts and blowing of horns they return singing "Summer-is-a-coming in" and dance on the green. Meanwhile friends greet friends and visit the various departments of Domestic Science, in charge of Miss Arnold', and there's also something about Strom Thurmond, whose name always sticks with me because it sounds like Lobster Thermidor, which is a dish that calls for washing head cavities in white wine. Anyway, it's a photo of the power of potential and is often proffered as evidence of something nice, but I'm not sure about that.

And finally: After she was married, Beezy sold her childhood home to the host of a public radio show about car upkeep, who was by all accounts a friendly but unrepentant drunk. While her house must have been pretty special, when it caught fire it *nearly set the whole goddamn forest alight.* Beezy had young children by then and had already traded down to our parents' childhood home, so she just put on her sunglasses, sat in a deckchair and watched the black smoke funnel upwards until it got dark. The fire trucks couldn't get in, you see. The house was set too far back and the road in was too far gone – what they call being hoisted with your own petard.

In the end Beezy's childhood home just burned to the ground.

12. Cemetery

We sat at the beginning of the woods and mulled over what Autumn had just told us.

'Now what?'

We couldn't risk going back the way we'd come. We were cut off.

'I don't want to go in the woods,' one of the littler ones said, and somehow that did it.

We all stood up and dusted off our laps and turned towards the forest's green, unknowable heart.

'What will you do with your eggs, Owen,' someone asked as we walked, 'eat them?' And Owen did a little half-start, which the crueller amongst us found diverting.

It was a question, though. It was clear by now that Owen had no intention of relinquishment, but how would he proceed through life with so fragile a cargo? We could picture him maybe with a special hard-shelled backpack full of Styrofoam peanuts or a glass box with velvet-lined, egg-shaped divots, though in either case he'd need logistical assistance from Pin. Pin herself was a mystery – a vast tundra punctured by the occasional shrub of her barking laugh – and of all the adults on that deck she had the greatest capacity for surprise. If any adult might indulge their son by financing the construction of a bomb-proof egg-vehicle, it was Pin.

Owen, we knew from Autumn, had started to pee himself on a fairly regular basis and had a rubber sheet under his normal cloth one, so maybe Pin would feel responsible and she'd let him get away with the eggs. That or she'd just chuck them out when they started to stink. There was no way of knowing.

The childhood home was whole minutes behind us and Frankie's house was somewhere to our left, we supposed, but we couldn't sense either anymore. The woods were woodsier than before, quieter. We called Abi and Travis's names only intermittently because our footsteps reverberated through the tented interior and did all the calling we could ask for and more. We were an absolute herd.

'Abi? Travis? Abi?'

'Travis?'

'Abi?'

Autumn stopped short and pointed.

'Trees,' she said, as if relaying new information.

But she was right, it *was* trees. Within the usual assortment of pines and beeches and oaks, there was a circle of different ones, papery and grey and arterial, like a bunch of saplings sewn together, but with big heavy arms that flopped back onto the ground. When we got closer we could see that they were covered with needles and smoky red glass beads. We recognised them as something we'd only ever seen trimmed into right angles and guarding banks and nursing homes, and so we knew what they spelled was *deliberation* and also *waiting patiently*.

One by one we slipped between their arms and entered a tiny field of stones, none of which came up higher than our knee. Someone had fought back the goldenrod and Queen Anne's Lace with clippers and the grass between the stones was tidy and uniform and there was a garden hose on a reel for keeping the grass nice, and overall it was a place someone clearly still cared for. The afternoon sun sifted through the leaves and lay over the cemetery in a gauzy sort of way. It was awfully still.

'Hello?' we announced ourselves across the clearing. We didn't want to give anything a fright and prompt it to act against our interests, I suppose. 'Hello? Hello?'

The stones did what they'd been doing, which was nothing, so we put one tentative foot into the ring of grass and then another until we were all amongst the stones, having a gander.

Despite sharing the quality of being fairly small, the stones varied in shape and style – some ornate, with little granite epaulets, and some plain – but all, you had the feeling, had been arranged by the same person, a person who was very much the captive of their own black moods and whims. Each stone had dates, some over a hundred years old and some fairly new, but all shockingly close together. The names were Dear Old Lady, Turk, Topsy, Hamish and Spinet, things like that. What it made us imagine was deceased puppets buried in cold soil, because what else – but, of course, it was really pets, though it took a good minute or two for this to dawn on us and, during those two minutes, we also entertained the possibility that it might be children, circus kids, with names that prevented them from joining society at large, hence the early deaths and ignominious backwoods burials.

At various points in our lives we had considered joining the circus, a daydream handed to us, in fact, by our parents. If we got mad and were casting around for something to do about it, our parents would suggest with great mirth that we run away to join the circus and eventually it became a concrete possibility in our minds, a genuine emergency hatch through which we could slip if things became too unbearable. Although we hadn't been to a circus, we had ideas of what it might entail: days of trundling along in painted wagons and stringing cooking pots over rosy fires and sitting in front of mirrors lit up by lightbulbs as large as conference pears, broken up by spurts of action in which we tested our fantastic discipline against the messy and somewhat arbitrary nature of death. I don't think it's something kids think about anymore and, anyway, we never did it. We stayed right where we were, which our parents always knew would be the case, which is why they'd offered it up like a dare in the first place. It was unkind but also their way of reaffirming the cords that bound us.

We were getting distracted again. In fact, we were so distractible it was getting worrying. The main thing holding our attention now were the two newest graves, cut from polished stone, the lettering etched and then painted in with gold paint. They were matching in that they looked the same and also in that they had the same dates: 09/1972 – 06/1980. The name on Grave One was Anatoli and the name on Grave Two was Mr B.

'Those were Beezy's Irish Settlers,' Autumn announced. 'The ones that died on the boat.'

We looked at Autumn, who was handing us new and valuable information twice in one hour, which was two times more than she had in her entire life.

'Please,' we said, 'explain.'

Autumn squinted into the soft, green canopy and shrugged. 'That's all I really know.'

It was unlike her to admit the limits of her knowledge and it gave her a sudden and unexpected depth.

'Come on,' we pressed, 'what else? What else do you know?'

'Well,' Autumn looked at the matching graves, 'I heard Aunt Maureen talking about Beezy's three-headed dogs, Anatoli and Mr B, and she said they're either in H-E-double-hockey-sticks or else waiting with the others, so this must be them.' We looked at the graves and thought about what it would be like to have three heads, even though we'd seen pictures of these dogs and they'd only had one apiece, or two if you added them up, but not three and definitely not six.

'And?'

'And when she died, Beezy tied them up on the boat and that's where they found them.'

This was phenomenal.

'*Tied* them?'

'Mm-hm, she tied both their leashes to her chair. And anyways dogs can swim, can't they, so otherwise they wouldn't have been there still.'

We didn't know. We didn't know the likelihood of the

dogs making it out alive from a wrecked sailboat, even if it was nested in a scurf of rocks, even if they were free to come and go as they pleased. People drown in much sillier circumstances. We pictured their sleek seal-like heads.

'Or maybe they were just loyal,' we ventured.

Autumn frowned and considered the possibility. In most of the pictures we'd seen, Beezy had a pair of dogs at her side, but they were never on leashes, no, they were there because they wanted to be, because life outside the perimeter of her reach was no life at all. As children this was the only kind of love we really recognised, the kind with no windows, like Kaspar Hauser in his little room, and if someone had opened the door and we were presented with a brilliant-green square of Bavarian foliage, would we have walked on out? No, I doubt it, I really highly doubt it.

We looked at the polished, trim graves, which seemed now like the advance guard of something. Autumn, in particular, stood over them, her black hair hanging down and around her face. The sun was nearly overhead. It sat on the ring of woods like a lid on a jar. And suddenly we were aware that we were confined to this little isle of neat grass, and though nothing stirred in the low, undulating limbs around us, we felt the shock of having inadvertently climbed up something very high. Autumn looked up from the graves but you could tell that her eyes were swimming, they couldn't quite rest on the shadowy world outside of our brilliant patch with its dangling particles of sunshine and all those bodies underneath.

What were we doing again? We were looking at things, these stones, each one with a name: Hamish, Spinet, Turk and Dear Old Lady, Anatoli and Mr B. We were thinking about the nature of loyalty and disloyalty.

We were very hot and still.

Was that it? Was that all?

Surely not. Surely we were looking for something. We had lost something and were here to retrieve it. We were here to bring it back home.

13. Cul-de-sac

What happened next was grisly, so let me just linger for a moment on the cemetery's garden hose:

The hose had a yellow stripe and we liked it a lot. It had a purpose, I suppose. We picked up the nozzle, which was like the head of an animal with its ears pressed flat back, and swung it. The hose looped through a reel and then connected to a spigot at the grass's edge. We touched the spigot's metal and it was cold, as if it had been run only just minutes ago. It was soothing to hold on to that hose, connected to a spigot and then by whatever cool, long pipe to the reservoir where some of our dads caught trash fish, for which you needed a $25 annual licence from the town hall. We thought about our town hall, which was next to a shop which stocked things from distant countries, and there was also paid parking. Then we thought about the Chinese restaurant just a couple doors down that sold Shirley Temples and the gas station staffed with teen-agers who washed your windshield whether you asked for it or not. It was good to think about the town, and more than one of us touched that spigot with the back of our hand and wished we were there. In that moment we would have traded every last Oh Henry! for a Hoodsie Cup from the chest freezer near the gas station counter – what I'm saying is that we wanted to pack it all in.

Autumn looked at the position of the sun and then held her watch up to the sky and pressed some buttons, frowning with concentration.

'It's,' she announced, pulling her lip, 'two-three-eight.'

Really, we thought, this is how people die. We touched the spigot and squinted through the zoetrope of green and thought about home, concerned more for ourselves at this point than either Abi or Travis. I worry that's what did it. Or maybe it's what some of us claimed later, that just in the moment before, we'd heard the not-too-distant shush of a car. But even if we'd seen the road—

'Guys!' The voice was not ours. It came from our left, just outside the ring of trees.

—even if we'd seen the road, it would not have made any material difference in the end.

It was Travis's voice, clear as day.

'Travis!' We overspilled the bounds of ourselves.

'Guys!'

Travis's cavalry sounded the bugle just beyond the ridge, molten, on-the-cusp, its intonation loose as always, slightly bored. Over the gravestones we leapt, the hose forgotten. Oh, he must have been right behind us the whole time! Travis who wore antiperspirant, who could whistle with a blade of grass—

'Travis, we're coming!'

—who always agreed to be a horse whenever Abi asked, not all brothers would do that—

'Guys! Just a minute!'

109

—but Travis did.

We flung ourselves through those sad, grey, heavy-armed trees and, on the other side, within a stone's throw of the little graves, was a hitching post with a great brass ring.

'Guys!'

The hitching post's ring was threaded through with vines and, behind it, a house-sized expanse of new growth, dense and woolly with ragweed and sumac, broken into plateaus, the sky overhead open, the sun hot. We stopped and scanned the expanse.

'Just a minute, guys!' Travis's voice was distinct but we simply could not see him.

'Travis, where are you!'

And amongst the brush, sections of wall – rosy brick sunken into long depressions or collapsed sideways, nothing joining up or making any sense, nothing higher than our shoulder. Under our sneakers, layered beneath the usual network of roots, were tectonic plates of greying cement, bent black nails, splinters of ceramic.

'Travis?'

As our eyes tried to locate Travis's voice amongst the remains, it hit us: this was Beezy's house. You probably already had that figured, though. The one that had burned to nearly nothing before we were born.

The sun shone.

Normally, in a place like this, the bugs would be going crazy, but the only sound was Travis. We called his name a few more times and then we just stood there and watched.

'Guys! Just a minute!'

Over the past few months Travis's voice had dropped, but unlike other boys his age, he hadn't seemed embarrassed. Even when it squeaked he'd just rolled his eyes. Now this newly deep voice oscillated through the undergrowth, nattering away about *minutes* and *waiting*. The cones of sumac and ragweed nodded imperceptibly. Hands in pockets, we watched Travis's voice, and in a peculiar way it was peaceful. A little bit like when you sit under a table and half-listen to what's being said above you, only this voice was everywhere: first over the far side of a wall, next from within a barrow of prickers. Sliding this way and that, that way and this, there but not really, tracing the ruined lines of the house. And the more we watched the less we thought about spigots and roads. A minute passed. And then all thoughts of Abi and Travis followed suit. It was nice. And then lastly any thoughts of ourselves. Us on the fulcrum, hands in pockets, quiet and easeful, ready to be tipped into sleep. A baby wrapped in a cloth. A person freezing to death.

The sun shone.

Then I suppose what happened is that we stopped watching and simply *saw*: the beams of sunlight arranging themselves into a lattice of actual beams, and through them the greeny shadows annealing, sharpening. The house, splendid and whole, rising up around us. Beezy's house – portico dressed in ivy, windows as tall as doors, with each darkened room beyond a polished slab of obsidian. Perfect. And there were no people in the house and that was perfect too; there were never meant to be.

Not even Travis, because the volume on his voice was cranked down suddenly, impatiently – and in its place a silence so loud, if you were an eardrum you'd leak. The most titanic silence you ever heard, trimmed to the very dimensions of the house. Our eyes rolled upwards, past the bristling chimneys, to the sun.

The sun looked back.

We stared, mouths open.

But

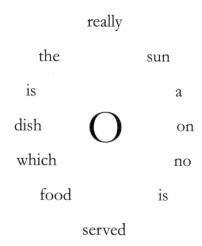

really

the   sun

is   a

dish   O   on

which   no

food   is

served

Bebeep! We blinked. Autumn.

Bebeep! Autumn's watch! Like a bird outside the window.

Bebeep! A bird who wanted everyone to wake up—

Autumn looked down at her watch like she'd forgotten she had a wrist, shook it slowly, then turned the alarm off.

'Shorry,' she said, her tongue heavy in her mouth, 'shorry.'

Black spots had eaten their way into our vision. There was a ringing in our ears. We rolled our shoulders, stiff like we'd gotten out of bed after an illness, our arms and faces tight and tender, a burn crept under our tans. How long had we been there? Oh, years and years. The area around us was shrunken again like a mouth without teeth, the brick retreating into the scrub.

The ringing dwindled and under the ringing there was the voice – but misshapen now, pliable, like it needed batteries, and we did not say a thing while it called to us, whatever it was. Oh God. Just a voicebox buried in a toy chest while the toy itself lies miles away. And our chests fizzed and our tongues went huge, which is what Frankie used to call 'the horrors', and we walked backwards, stiffly, away from the broken house and Travis's broken voice, and we were in the little cemetery again with its millimetre-high grass and laughing particles of sunshine and not-Travis's awful voice unspooling in the heat between us, and then someone threw a rock and that someone was Owen.

'Jaast a minaat guyees!'

The rock punched a hole in the greenery, letting off a syrupy smell, and before it had time to close itself, another rock sailed through.

The next one was hippo-snouted and carried with it clods of dirt.

Owen let it fly, his babies balanced along his other arm.

'Guyees!' A note of desperation had crept into its voice after the second or third rock, like someone approaching the end of a long joke they'd forgotten the punchline to, and Owen winged a pebble at one of the headstones and the voice's register crept higher, and Owen threw a bigger rock at another headstone and it made a good smacking sound and the voice started up faster, 'OKeeguysOKeeguys!', and then we all went berserk. We kicked and kicked at those headstones, and if we could have torn them up with our teeth we would have done that too: it was the only option available to us, really the only one, we had to show it that we did not care, that after everything it had put us through, *we did not give a shit.*

'Guys!' it pumped out one last time, releasing a raw green syrupy smell, and then it was gone. Possibly it wanted us to think it was gone. Maybe it had folded itself up under a nearby rock and was regarding us with a single eye, but in the moment we weren't bothered anymore, we just kept jumping off headstones and trying to rock them off their foundations. A few of us started spitting, really letting gobs of saliva drip from our mouths onto the graves. I can see how sometimes these things get out of hand and people do things they regret. The force of our hate was a kite on the end of a very long string: you could tie it to a fencepost and it would stay up all night.

So we were aping it up all over the gravestones but it couldn't go on for ever. Eventually it wound down and we were doubled over, panting and thrilling to our small victory, and that's when we saw that, while we'd been trying to decimate the cemetery, Owen had been building something. It was a pile of stones, one on top of the other, and it was about the height of the gravestones, but with none of the flash and polish. His tongue stuck out of the corner of his mouth as he balanced the last few and the pile swayed but held itself upright. It was especially difficult because one arm was taken up with his eggs, and we all held our breath while the structure decided whether it wanted to fall. We watched him as he did the last stone and stood back.

One time an uncle showed us an incredible number of pictures of a family trip to Scotland and the only one that stayed with us was a picture of a small island that was more like a hunk of land torn from the cliffs behind it. It was tall and worn away with barely any grass and the whole thing was just covered in little and big towers of stones. Covered! That's where Owen had gotten his idea, sure, it must have been, but what exactly it symbolised was as foggy to us as it was clear to him. We liked it anyway. We approved.

'That's cool, Owen,' we said, and Owen nodded and looked quietly pleased. It *was* cool, and actually now Owen was cool too. If Owen won big at Majestic Sands, he wouldn't have kept a penny of it, that was for sure, he would have given it out in fistfuls until every last bit was gone.

'That's so cool, Owen.' Autumn clomped over and put her arm around Owen's puny exoskeleton.

We looked at the stone tower again and it was nice, it was good to make our mark. If we could have, we would have built the tower high enough to look out over the tree-tops; that would have been really excellent, something so high it would be visible from the centre of town with its two white spires, something you could see from the gas station and town hall and even the Chinese restaurant, where diners would peer up at our tower between mouthfuls of fluorescent chicken.

Autumn knelt before the tower. Around us the pine trees gave off their smell and the sunlight rushed down and the gravestones were as keenly devoted to death as ever, but we didn't pay any of that attention as we looked.

'Wow, Owen,' we repeated, 'that is really cool,' and at this moment Autumn withdrew something from her pocket and placed it on the top stone. The tower quaked but held.

We couldn't see what Autumn had placed on the very top until she turned to us like *ta da*, and sitting there was Abi's hair thing with its stars and its infinite feedback loop.

Oh, you won't understand it now, but it was an abomination. We were incensed. It was hard to explain at the time, and is still hard to explain, but all I can tell you is that Owen had done a beautiful and right thing, his gesture was redemptive and correct and unexpected and original, and through a heady combination of dopiness and cheap sentimentality, Autumn had turned it into another gravestone.

We pushed back from Autumn and she stood there, receding, holding her smile out to us, but we did not want it *at all*.

'Where,' someone said, 'did you get that?'

Autumn's smile wavered but held. She *was* getting fat: it was obvious to us now, we could see it even as we pulled away.

'It's Abi's,' she said, covered in cow-like incomprehension, 'remember?'

'But Travis had it,' someone else pointed out. 'He put it in his pocket.'

Autumn shook her head and her lovely black hair moved around her face, which was lumpen with hurt.

'No,' she was starting to look a little wild, 'I found it, I found it hanging on the spout! I meant to say but I forgot.' And, oh, who did she take us for? The hair thing should not have been there. It just really should not.

'Give it back,' we said, though to whom we didn't specify. Dear Old Lady and Spinet and that whole lot twitched their dead ears upwards.

Autumn took a step back and the tower trembled and she looked at us and then spun around to give it back, I suppose. I think that's what she was meaning to do, but instead the tower listed and spilled itself all over the grass and we shouted 'No!' in a way whose drama matched the moment. Autumn dropped to her knees and scrabbled, issuing a confused and running apology, and tried to hand us the hair thing and gather up the stones at the same time, and of course none of it worked, and so we just watched her like we were distant cogs in the Mechanic's celestial machine and she was just pecking around in the dirt. Owen stood behind Autumn with his two babies still in one arm and with the other he pulled at her t-shirt, only very lightly, and said her name, but Autumn was a spinning top veering this way and that until she sprang up suddenly and she shouted, 'There! Just *have* it!' and simply *chucked* the hair thing at us, her elbows flying out like plucked wings, and that's when it happened, the worst thing – tied for the worst but in many ways the very worst thing.

A succulent crack.

Owen, stopped still in the sun, his chin tucked tight against his 'I Won Big at Majestic Sands' t-shirt.

'Owen!' We rushed at him.

And over his arm and down and down his t-shirt, delicate fingernails of blue and white caught in a jellied river.

'Oh no!' We couldn't countenance it. 'Owen, your egg!'

It was too horrible. Some of us averted our gaze and some of us tried to scrape away the yolk in a respectful kind of manner, and one of us took the surviving egg and held it up to the light and we murmured and fretted without touching him, but none of us were big enough to do what probably needed to be done in that moment.

'Oh, Owen,' we whispered, 'your egg.'

Owen did not meet our eye.

And what did the forest do? Nothing at all. It didn't seem happy or sad, no tittering or wagging. The entirety of the forest just sat there, regarding.

'Oh, Owen, your poor egg.'

We placed the remaining egg in his hand and closed his dirty little fingers around it and we said, 'There, there you go, at least you got this one,' all the while knowing it was an awful thing to say.

And as for Autumn, where was she?

Autumn was alone and walking backwards. Her elbow dripped a little. The hammock of leaves swayed overhead.

We turned to her.

'Autumn, you barfbag.'

Her face quavered.

'You spaz.'

And then she wheeled around so she was facing the heart of the forest and fled, punching through the greenery like a rock.

'Oh shit,' someone said, and we all shook our heads except for Owen, because Owen was through the tear Autumn's velocity had created before it even had time to mend.

14. A Third Revelation

The boughs wagged shut. Owen and Autumn were gone.

'Oh shit.'

We ran too. We had no choice.

'There!' We could see Owen's red t-shirt disappearing at top speed through the scrub.

We were running so fast we forgot to feel mad. We ran downhill through the forest, fleetly, as we called *Owen Autumn Autumn Owen*, always with Owen's little red t-shirt nipping from view and everything else one long smear of green. Because we were running downhill and we were scared, we were faster than we'd ever been before but so, of course, were Owen and Autumn, all of us just flying, just flying through the trees, hurtling through the scrub. *Hallooo! Halllloooooooo!!!!*

When I said Autumn possessed surprising speed, I meant it. You wouldn't have guessed, not in a million years, but Autumn aced the Presidential Fitness Test footraces every year, though her agility wasn't much to write home about. If you asked her to change direction, forget about it. Basically she barrelled – squat, long-haired Autumn – through friend and foe alike.

Hallooooo!

Autumn and Owen and Owen and Autumn. *Halloo!*

We cantered over a log. It felt wonderful to run.

Because we weren't thinking about what was behind us or what was lying in wait, but just letting ourselves be carried along and wanting to catch Owen and clutch him to our breast like an egg, but also not wanting, really, to get yolk all over ourselves, we missed what was right there. It was a hole.

'Whoa!' someone shouted, and teetered, and we all nearly pushed them in, but we managed to get a hold of their shirt and yank them back just at the last second.

'Whoa.'

The hole's diameter was a few inches wider than the tallest amongst us. We backed away from its lip and looked. It was impossible to determine how deep it was because it didn't seem deep at all. In fact, it didn't seem much like a hole to the untrained eye. It was closer to a blanket laid over a hole, a membrane of orange pine needles and tufty pebbles and all the usual sort of thing, but ever so slightly raised and sunken at the same time, like a picture of a hole in one of those *Magic Eye* books which hadn't even been created yet. I only knew about them later because I kept receiving them over and over for every birthday and Christmas.

Did you know that the first *Magic Eye* book was published in Japan and its original title was *Your Eyesight Gets Better & Better in a Very Short Rate of Time*? Well, they were right, that's exactly what had happened, our eyesight had gotten better in a very short rate of time. We looked at the hole and were overcome with the conviction that the forest wanted us to walk right into it and get swallowed up for ever, and all the newspapers would talk about how our poor parents didn't even have a body to bury. But not today.

We threw a handful of pine needles onto the hole and it flinched. Someone threw a stick and the stick landed very heavily, like an iron bar. The hole didn't know how to behave and it was funny, actually, we were feeling so puffed up, actually, so eagle-eyed, that it took us a full minute or so to hear a wet sort of whimpering.

We cocked our heads. There it was again. We looked down.

Owen at the bottom of the hole. Oh, we couldn't bear it; it wasn't even the kind of hole with a bottom.

We dropped to our knees and leaned closer but the sound emanating from the hole was this: static, which could have just been the dry ground crunching beneath our bodies, but, no, I don't think it was, I think it was the hum of a TV between channels. Up close, the pine needles had an iodine smell. The whole thing was odious in the extreme but we could at least say that the whimpering was not coming from the hole and our relief was astronomical. We stood up and listened harder.

The whimpering was like a cat, if a cat really wanted you to feel bad about, say, not feeding it.

'Autumn!'

We edged around the hole with care and there, behind a tree, was Autumn. She was holding her ankle and of course she was the source of the moaning, and bundled in next to her was Owen and his egg and our hearts were jubilant and huge.

'I hurt my ankle.' Autumn looked up at us all with her giant black eyes and, for a short moment, pity trembled in our hearts like a drop of rain on a windowpane before it broke apart and slid away. 'I fell,' she said, 'back there.' And she pointed behind us to the hole.

Back where? We turned our heads towards the hole as if we didn't know what she was referring to. Back there? We weren't focusing so much on Autumn as thinking about Owen and his baby being alive and well and not in a hole.

Autumn nodded.

'A rabbit's hole, I think. It really hurts. It wouldn't let me go.'

And then Autumn looked up at us all, weighing whether we could be trusted, and then decided to do it anyway. She uncupped her hands from around her leg. A gasp flowed through the circle. Delicate cuts, perfectly straight and regular, ran every quarter inch around her ankle like the lines of an elasticated ankle sock. They were so fine, these cuts, that we could barely see them, there wasn't any blood to speak of, it was as if the skin had been sliced just so. Perforated.

'Yuck, Autumn,' we said, 'grody.'

Shame budded on Autumn's face, but we'd never seen anything like it and what would you have said?

'I told you,' Autumn's hands closed back around her ankle, her lustrous hair drew shut, 'it wouldn't let go.'

Autumn, it was clear, was at the end of the line. We drummed our fingers and traced our initials in the dirt and clicked our tongues. Owen's knees were almost up to his ears and he held his egg in both hands and his eyes looked baggier. Once in a while he brought the remaining egg up close to his nose and breathed on it, *huff huff.* The egg looked lonely and important at the same time, which is often the case with only children.

He never once looked down at his shirt, though. I don't think he could.

'Listen, Autumn,' we said after a while, 'we can't just stay here all day, you know.' That foul, buzzing hole was too close.

We made a tight circle and surveyed the top of Autumn's black head.

'I'm not going,' her hair said. 'Just leave me.'

We exchanged a look. Without Autumn there would be no Owen.

'We'll walk slow,' we promised. 'We'll give you the rest of the Oh Henry!s, you can choose TV when we're back, Owen will let you choose the TV for a month.' But it was to no avail. The long black hair swung stubbornly back and forth.

'We need to find Abi,' we tried, 'and Travis. They'll be wondering where we are. Come on, Autumn.'

Autumn's hair went still but she didn't move, it was no use, and then one enterprising soul, the one of us who would go on to make quite a lot of money, actually, in agribusiness tech, said, 'Autumn, look, what would Travis do?', and that of all things did it, because of course it would. It was cheap, though, as a ploy.

Autumn's hair parted. We could see the red nub of her face peering upwards, blinking, deciding. Then she opened her mouth and took in a long, black breath and the words spurted upwards from her throat like she was a fountain someone had finally remembered to turn on:

'*Travis* is the one who hurt *Abi* in the first place.'

The words hung there about her head, frozen. The whole forest leaned in.

'What?' the agribusiness cousin finally said. They were angry, their composure falling off them in sections.

Autumn looked at all of us, one at a time, puckered and defiant. Hurt jiggled behind her eyes.

'Well, it's true!' she yelled. 'Owen was there too, weren't you, Owen? You saw it too, didn't you, Owen?'

We looked at Owen, who tucked his chin and nodded, and we all died a little inside, or at least any future flowering was less glorious than it would have been if Autumn had just kept her mouth shut. Here is what she told us:

Autumn told us that Travis had done something really terrible at school.

We tightened the circle despite ourselves. Doing something terrible at school was something that intrigued us.

On the last day of school – *Travis's* last day of school, that is, me and Owen were at Aunt Maureen's for the day because Mom was at work and—

Yes? we urged.

Travis had written something about another boy on the windowsill at school. It was something bad, and whatever it was had made Aunt Maureen cry right there and then. The principal called and she had to go in. Travis got sent up to his room and, when Aunt Maureen got back, she cried some more. Me and Owen were sitting on the top of the stairs.

What was it?

Something really terrible. No one would say. And then Aunt Maureen said Travis was expulsed.

And?

And then Travis cried and said he wasn't sure why he'd . . . why he'd done it. He was a change student, the boy Travis wrote about.

Exchange student?

Yes, and Aunt Maureen said she was *ashamed* and that Travis had *let her down* and that he had *let himself down* also, and Travis was in his room crying. And then we saw Abi go in his room and then Travis told her to get out, but she was like that sometimes.

Abi can be annoying.

Annoying. Yes. She was just little and annoying. So he just took her arm and dragged her out, but she was twisting around and screaming, and Travis said *sorry sorry sorry* and you could tell that he really was sorry but it didn't matter, they had to take her to the hospital.

Christ.

We were there on the stairs but they forgot about us, they forgot about us and—

And?

—and then me and Owen waited outside until dinnertime for Mom.

Autumn's hair closed back over her face.

We sat and weighed the new knowledge Autumn and Owen had gifted us, unforgivably awful and now ours.

We were so busy turning things over in our heads —
Travis's yellow flag of hair and pocked neck, Abi's purple
cast and, underneath, a very sticky, soft, broken arm, the
tic tac toe which ended, as it almost always does, in a tie —
that we missed it. Owen's egg, superb and fine and blue,
giving off the kind of light that passes through a really
thin white cup in a sunny kitchen, sitting in Autumn's
palm. It was obvious even to us that the egg had been
freely given, and though Autumn's face was mottled with
recent crying, the expression itself was clear. Owen's egg
was Autumn's daughter now.

Owen's hands were working themselves a little,
coming to terms with their new emptiness. Brother
and sister sat up against the trunk and then Autumn
took Owen's hand and held it — while we took measure
of our new situation, what they looked most like was a
pair of scales finding their balance. And it was only
after we all got up, Autumn helping Owen and Owen
helping Autumn, the rest of us fending for ourselves,
that we first noticed Autumn's watch. We noticed that
it was gone.

Autumn's watch had simply disappeared.

15. Intermezzo: Weakness

Beezy didn't like birthdays and she didn't like weakness either. But my feeling is that, whereas before her illness she found weakness deplorable, after the illness she found it funny. It was the sort of humour you could get out of an old-fashioned clown with open-top shoes and turned-out pockets. A humourless kind of humour. Or maybe it's the essence of humour, maybe humour is braided with misfortune and if it's not tragic it's not funny. Either way, it would explain a lot, especially some of the things that happened in the days leading up to the wreck and Beezy's death and all that rigmarole.

Even though Frankie was the one who hung around for years taking care of her, I can't imagine Beezy was grateful. In fact, Beezy told anyone who would listen that Frankie was the most incurious person she'd ever met. Beezy also thought that Frankie was a bigot because Frankie had voted for Nixon right out of high school, which our parents said was a bit rich, all things considering. Conversely, Frankie thought each and every one of us should be a city upon a hill.

Incurious. It made me think a little of the picture in Frankie's barn of all the kids with their shining foreheads and whether there was one, maybe, whose forehead shone less brightly, a dullard at the edges, but I'm nearly sure they all looked more or less the same. Like they were full of oxygen and sunlight. When I think of them together, Beezy and Frankie, I think of Beezy sitting in her chair in a throne-like sort of way with her crown of white flowers and Frankie in attendance with her ski-jump nose and all her yellow hair spilling out of a giant banana clip, and the expression on Beezy's face is this: annoyance.

Because Frankie was maybe the last person Beezy should have lived with if you took it from Beezy's point of view. Frankie was not only unfunny in a traditional sense, but she could ride a horse backwards and hotwire a car and put up a stud wall and her only weakness, that we could see, was her unyielding devotion to Beezy, which aggravated Beezy to no end. For Frankie, life was an otherwise shallow tray of water.

One Memorial Day, not long before Beezy died, Frankie invited family and some horse friends over for dinner at our parents' childhood home, where she was living while she cared for Beezy, and later on Beezy couldn't stop telling everyone how Frankie had served *lasagne and salad*. What irked her most of all were the breadsticks, which were passed around in their box. Aunt Maureen was there with Uncle Steve, and they did that line together:

'Their *box*.'

Also Frankie's horse friends were mostly golfers and had a golfer's sensibility about life, and so talked a lot about property prices and made jokes at the expense of the Barbadian home aids who cared for their own elderly parents, and referred to President Carter as the

Peanut Farmer, and what Aunt Maureen said was that Beezy looked like a goldfish planning to jump from her bowl.

'The thing was,' Aunt Maureen explained, 'they were all just fairly *nice* people – their politics were excruciating but they were pleasant enough, and also they were Frankie's *friends*, for Pete's sake, they'd been *invited*.'

So conversation was about whatever and it was nearly over, maybe a round of Folgers to come, but everyone was mentally preparing themselves for the end when a spoon sounded against a glass and they all turned to Beezy, who was sat at the head of the table.

Beezy was sorry for interrupting such *stimulating* intercourse – in the retelling, Aunt Maureen had held up a glass and done the whole thing with the glass and the spoon – but it seemed that she had *soiled* herself and so she was off to bed.

It put a real end to the evening.

'I hadn't seen Beezy so delighted in years,' Aunt Maureen finished. 'She laughed all the way to her room.'

But had she? We were desperate to know. *Had she soiled herself?*

No one would ever tell us and, to be honest, I think they couldn't remember because to them it wasn't germane. It didn't matter because the punchline was that she had *said* it, but to us who were still within the borders of childhood, it mattered very much, to us it was the nub.

Anyway, the point is that Frankie's unyielding competence and good spirits drove Beezy right up the wall:

Here is Frankie singing 'Raindrops on Roses' as she carries Beezy to the bath.

Here is Frankie sticking a Christmas ribbon to Beezy's cardigan and whispering, 'God bless us, every one.'

I can't say that these things definitely happened but I can guess that they probably did.

Whereas Pin was tough as nails and Aunt Maureen had her little nest of ambitions, and the boys were a moot point because they were far away, Frankie was entirely cutaneous. You could make her cry at the drop of a hat and what fun was that? What Beezy might have found funny was the Mechanic, but that all came after. Yes, I think Beezy might have really liked the sight of Frankie ghosting around in black, but Beezy denied herself that chance, and my opinion is that's the risk you run when you decide to kill yourself.

The sailboat was the one thing that Frankie didn't keep of Beezy's because it was too far gone and also, of course, a terrible reminder. It was little and black and nearly fifty years old, but first our grandfather, then Beezy, then Frankie had kept it in excellent working order, and on sunny and calm days Frankie took Beezy out, lifting onto the deck her body and then her chair and then hypothetically also her spirits. Sometimes Frankie brought a picnic, but most often it was just Saltines and ginger ale. Years after Beezy's death, Frankie talked about what fantastically jolly times they had manoeuvring around headlands and waving to passing craft. She showed us photos:

Here is Beezy in an orange life vest and tweed slacks

taking some sun. With her short hair and leathery skin, her top half looks like a walking stick and her bottom half is mostly hidden by a blanket.

Here is Travis, knee-high, white-blond, standing next to Beezy, who is seated at the helm, and the angle of the picture means the mast sprouts up right from her skull. Beezy's hand is resting on Travis's head, her first grand-child and, as far as she ever knew back then, her only one. They're both looking at the camera but you can't tell much from their eyes because they're squinting. Behind them you can just see very bright light over very cold-looking water.

'We were planning on taking a long trip,' Frankie would tell us with her tiny welling eyes, 'just the two of us. Oh, kids, she would have *loved* that.'

'But if she couldn't stand Frankie,' we asked our parents, 'why didn't she hire a nurse? Or live in a home?'

Our parents looked at us and shook their heads. *No*, they told us, *that would have been impossible, Beezy never would have allowed it.* And that's all they would say on the subject.

I don't know if she drowned or was just bashed on the head, but the oddest thing about when they found her was not how she got to the harbour in the first place or that she was still in her chair and not even that Anatoli and Mr B were still with her but that she was in the *cabin* of the boat, which you could only access by a *hopelessly narrow* set of stairs.

'How in the world?' I imagine the men from the coast-guard saying, brandishing their flashlights, seeing the woman, the chair, the dogs, everything in the half-dark, half-floating. 'What in holy hell?'

It would have been bad for someone, it would have made the news and all sorts if they hadn't found Beezy's affairs – the will, the manuscript, her personal correspondence – in perfect order, arranged only the week before by Beezy herself, as affirmed by her lawyer, if anything in a state of extreme cheer. Our parents' childhood home, I think, went to Frankie on the condition that she would sell it off post haste, and the cache of awful old stuff was to be divided up by her children using their judgement, which is clearly just chum in the water.

Whichever way you look at it, a level-headed person could only draw the conclusion that Beezy had killed herself on purpose and so *that* was *that*. Only of course no one, literally no one, in the family would let it go. Considering everything, you'd assume they'd forget it with absolute abandon. They could have thrown some flowers out to sea and maybe even strong-armed the local paper into one of those more detailed obituaries that they dress up as news, and then gone home and put their feet up and cast around for something decent to watch. But you never can tell, you never did know: Chuck Berry had it exactly right.

It's a nice song, that Chuck Berry one, if you listen to the lyrics. Despite Chuck Berry's personal failings, it's still a really lovely song.

16. No Man's Land

'Maybe the hole snatched it when I pulled out my foot.'

We looked back over our shoulders and there was nothing but a blanket of pine needles.

'Sorry, Autumn,' we said, not feeling sorry enough to dig around in the hole for her watch.

First Owen's egg and now this. There were no two ways about it – we were beat. Our options, as we saw them, had narrowed until all we could think to do was walk, and whereas earlier in the afternoon our legs thought about trying to go home, now they didn't. Where they wanted to go now was downhill. Gravity maybe, or inertia, the mark you make when you let the chalk in your hand pull itself down a chalkboard, a marble in a marble tilt. Also, I suppose, at the backs of our minds there was always the river.

Autumn limpered and clasped the egg, which was her daughter now. Owen, empty-handed, pinned to her side. The forest guided us down.

As we walked we mulled over Travis's costly school. We thought about all the robots Travis would never build, the sailing trips he would have to witness from the shore. We pictured the principal who'd cast him out, filling the doorway of the wood-panelled office with his finger pointed in the direction of anywhere but there, out into the catastrophic darkness of other, lesser institutions. Travis, who had been our firmament, half-ignoring us, a distracted hand on our head cementing our endless devotion.

Had they painted it over, whatever he'd written? They would have had to if it was so bad. So vile you'd tell a person never to come back. We thought of the things written on the walls of our own schools and shuddered.

Most of us weren't calling for Travi and Abis anymore. Autumn was, though. She limpered and called:

'Abi! Travis!'

Someone pointed out that it would be dinner in a couple of hours. We hadn't even had lunch. The agribusiness cousin took a flattened Oh Henry! from a pocket and started to eat, and so most of us withdrew an Oh Henry! from our own pockets. Besides Hansel and Gretel, we also associated stray candy with razorblades and hallucinogens, though later we found out that kind of thing never really happened, strangers putting stuff in kids' candy. Like 'Hansel and Gretel', in fact, it was nearly always the parents.

The chocolate had melted against the warmth of our thighs but we ate it anyway, mindlessly. Not Owen and Autumn, though. I suppose they were full. We were in various stages of consummation when the late afternoon sun started to loosen the foliage, the branches lifting and lightening, the ground levelling, and there we were, having travelled so far down, further than we'd ever permitted ourselves, the branches parted ahead of us and we found ourselves at a tennis court.

We stopped and lowered our candy and, in our depleted state, we thought the very thought you're thinking now, which is *enough already*.

Unlike the baggy chain-link and rotting acrylic of your average tennis court, this one was pristine and unfenced and made of grass. The grass was the length of our fingernail and dense and ribboned with deep green. The net was taut and there wasn't a single leaf or acorn that we could see, no equipment leaning up against trees, no shed or path, no spigot. The light landed very softly.

The court was pristine but it also felt recently occupied; we were attuned now, our nose in the air. Here is what it was like: it was like coming across a haughty woman with no clothes on strolling across her lawn in the early morning, like you're just a perverted squirrel in the bushes and that's why she's doing it in the first place. You're just the prop and the audience and the fall-guy rolled into one.

We walked up to the white line and drew a toe along it. The pattern of white squares was freshly done. It took us a minute to see that they had been swapped round, the single square laid out at the net, the double squares back at the baseline. It was odd but no biggie. The paint was so white we half-thought it would come off on our sneakers, but it stayed right where it was. The grass was cushiony and succulent and walking on it felt like finding your feet on a boat. We bounced on our heels, we knelt and ran our hands along its miraculous surface.

'A racquet!' Someone held up not one but two racquets, wooden ones with cane faces and stippled leather grips and necks striped in gloss paint in the colours of the Harvard Club or some other esoteric rat hole.

'And some balls.' Another cousin held up a red-and-white can.

The racquets were new and the can still sealed. I can't remember who twisted the key but it wasn't me, though it might have been. The sound of the can opening was a slicing sound, silvery and clean, and the odour of the balls – wool, rubber and glue – was so strong it knocked all other thoughts out of our heads. It was the smell of industry and hale fellowship. Under our shoes the grass contracted and then loosened with anticipation.

We shouldn't have done it, precisely because we were meant to, because it so clearly wanted us to, but we were tired and badly disabused and what happened next does not say great things about us. What I think happened is that, after the awful shock administered by Autumn and Owen, we really just wanted to be *cut some slack*.

'Shall we?'

Two of us out on the lawn, lobbing the ball in arcs under the clearing's appreciative blue eye. We played badly, laughing, chasing missed shots to the edge of the court, where they always slowed their roll to just where the grass ran out. They never left the court, of course, those balls, they simply couldn't. And most of the rest of us cheering them on, shouting sportsmanlike things, like 'Hey, batta batta batta' and 'Ooooo, another one bites the dust!' Then someone else would run out onto the court and muscle a player aside, saying it was their turn, and the first player would relinquish their racquet with none of the usual resentment, with gladness even; yes, they would say, *have a turn, it's really pretty great*, and the replacement player would pick up where their ancestor had left off, swinging like an absolute idiot, doing exaggerated dives, having a blast.

And it was really pretty great because suddenly everything else – Travis's transgressions, Abi's little arm, Owen's egg and Autumn's watch, all the disappearances and nursed grievances, the very porous and wilful nature of our environment – was forgotten. We were made to forget them, I think, and also we very much wanted to.

And the more we played the better we got, each new pair of players faster and more confident. On a normal day we were not tennis people, the most we could claim was ping pong – we were not the exalted children of Marblehead, for instance, with their culottes and power serves. Travis, maybe, was meant to be a tennis person. If he had wanted, I'm sure his school offered all that kind of thing; he could have been a tennis person if he hadn't screwed up so very badly. But now, at this very moment, we were swift and possessed incredible economy of motion and we knew, you see, that our aim was true before contact was even made. Our minds had started to calculate backspin and dropshots at such tremendous speed that we became a convincing simulacrum of animals who did everything beautifully and without thought. Our rallies were endless. The sun was back directly overhead. I remember because there were no shadows on the court.

We were entranced.

And the better we played, the less we clowned, because it wasn't funny anymore and it really wasn't much of a game anymore either. It was the kind of fear that keepy-uppy engenders but on a very large and perhaps ugly scale, where the consequences are imaginary and therefore boundless. We were balletic in our play and we all felt with a conviction that was both sudden and primordial that our bond was our strength or something along those lines, and the next thing we knew we had shoved Autumn and Owen onto the court. Autumn and Owen who had been silent for the duration of our tournament, who had been, for the first time that afternoon, practically invisible. The two players on the court slowed their game, waiting for their replacements, but the siblings stood half-in, half-out.

They simply gawped at us.

'Take your turn,' we urged. 'It's your turn now.'

They didn't say a thing.

'You must,' we suggested.

And then Owen shook his head and, oh, this was too much. This was an outrage.

We were more than entranced, really – I suppose you would call us possessed.

'Go on,' we said, 'it's your turn now, take your turn.'

Autumn looked at us, one after the other, until she ran out of eyes to plead with, opening and closing her mouth, a fish hauling her awful body over land. Owen pushed his hands deep into his shorts. The sun had centred itself in the sky.

So much time wasted! We weighed the racquets in our hands and examined Autumn and Owen. All their minor concerns and predictable weak spots. The needless interruptions, the divorce, the handouts . . . the bedwetting! The feeling that had dogged us all day stepped out of the shade and stood transformed, distended, fully resplendent in the sun. And with new or perhaps very old eyes we could finally see Autumn and Owen for what they were. We licked our lips keenly:

Autumn and Owen were interlopers.

We walked them to the centre of the court, gimpy Autumn's head hanging right off her shoulders, fingers steepled over her adopted daughter. We held out the racquets very firmly and told them what fun they might have if they only agreed.

Then we stood back and waited for the game to begin.

Autumn raised her racquet, weakly it must be said, her daughter nesting in the palm of the other hand, and lifted the ball over the net to Owen. Owen did a little stumble towards the ball and it skidded off the rim of his racquet and flew over his shoulder and we hissed.

Autumn and Owen stood at the net and looked at us. 'Come on now,' we counselled. 'Just do your best, OK?'

Owen tried again, and this time he managed to balance the ball on the centre of his racquet and, with a spasm, he sent it over the net, but Autumn couldn't get to it on time. She took a few stilted steps towards where the ball had been and we clicked our tongues. She was really making a meal of it, the situation with her ankle and the egg. She looked at us as if to say *please*.

'Go on. Pick up the ball.'

Autumn picked up the ball. She tossed it into the air but it just fell back to earth like a dead bird. She tried again and the same thing happened.

'You're pathetic,' someone observed.

Autumn looked out at us and we hated her very much. She was a torment to all of us that we couldn't stand much longer.

'My ankle hurts,' she said, and we said, 'Go on.'

Autumn tried again. Finally she faltered up to the net and threw the ball underhand to Owen, who missed.

'Come *on*!' We were full of encouragement and hatred. All of our good work, the exemplary craftsmanship of our game, those meticulously webbed racquets, the immaculate balls. And we thought about a fact that we hadn't known we knew, we all thought at the very same time about how antecedents of tennis were played with bare hands, then hands wrapped in rope and then wooden bats. *We hadn't even needed racquets*, we thought to ourselves, we were really worked up, *once upon a time we played until our mitts were absolutely tenderised!*

I don't know how long it went on. Too long, obviously. It was like they were playing under heavy sedation in shin-deep sand, Autumn growing slower, grunting, the cape of her hair getting wet with effort and sticking to her neck, her collapsing gait, and though we could see what it was costing her, in our new, enhanced state that was fine, that was the manner of play. And Owen,

141

unmanly, covered in his own egg, mincing across the green, the sloughed skin of a failed enterprise. And when the two conferred at the net, we shrieked because now we saw what Owen was carrying: Autumn's egg for safekeeping, his little niece, an unearned reprieve.

It had been coming all day, we'd heard it on the tracks. In some ways it had been travelling towards us from the moment we'd stepped out of our cars and now the trees had parted and it was here.

'What time is it, Autumn?' we called. '*Time* to buy a new watch!'

We started to laugh. The laughter started outside of us, I'm sure of it. I would really like to say that that's true.

It was silvery and clean. It was polite and spiteful.

'Please,' Autumn said aloud.

It was the laugh of people in shade looking at people in the baking sun. Our laughter grew outwards and we started, of all things, to applaud. Autumn and Owen staggered around the court as if they had just been in some sort of dreadful car accident and we clapped our hands together and whistled.

'Good going, guys!'

'Awesome job!'

Owen wasn't crying, but Autumn was; but then she always was, it was nothing new. Only this time it was hilarious and also it really enraged us.

'You're sexy!' someone shouted, and Autumn turned her face away.

Autumn was really crying now, her oafish, dark body just absolutely convulsed, and she raised an unsound arm and tried again, her *nth* try, and we hallooed – it came right from our toes and we could have stormed the court, if it hadn't all been so funny to watch; we could have eliminated them from the game right there and then and we would have, I think. We definitely could have.

And maybe that's what did it, because in a small and private space burrowed far away from our screams a golden thread, the sort you tie to someone else so neither of you falls off a mountain, was being extended between brother and sister.

Autumn swung her arm back.

The ball sailed cleanly over the net and Owen ran for it this time with new intent and we knew, with an astonishment that maybe brought us partway back to ourselves, that he was going to make it. He ran with his racquet outstretched and he was smiling – even through our new old eyes, it was nice to see him smile – and then he slipped.

The thick green grass was just pulled out from under his feet and Owen went over, hard, onto his back, the racquet flying from one hand and the egg shooting forward from the other into the air, and Autumn running madly as if both her legs had never worked better and reaching out her arms and catching it, softly, her whole body bent in the catch.

Her whole dark body was bent around her catch and then she straightened and held out her hand and in it was the egg, blue and heavy.

'Owen, I've got it!' she called, the golden string between Autumn and Owen vibrated. 'I've got our egg!'

Autumn stood there with both hands cupped around the egg, a gift that became, with hindsight, new each time.

Owen lay on his back for a long while, his tiny ribcage pulsing under his 'I Won Big' t-shirt.

It was us who were invisible now. It was only the brother and sister left, and their string and their egg. We went quiet.

'Owen?' Autumn went up to the net.

We watched little Owen on the grass, breathing. His face was like a twist of paper you might throw into a fire to help it start.

After a minute or so Owen rolled over and, when he did, the stink was tremendous. It reached our nostrils all the way over on the sideline.

No one went to help him. I'm sorry for this, but no one did. Travis would have. Travis, despite his newly acquired unsightliness, wouldn't have let this happen in the first place. You had, at least, to give him that.

Owen picked himself up and examined himself disinterestedly. He looked at the bottom of each of his shoes, which were caked in shit. Shit ran up the backs of his hairless legs.

'It's from a dog,' he said to himself.

It was. We could see it there, a huge red dog turd smeared across the middle of Owen's side of the court, where none had been before. The white eye above the clearing winked and that's when I knew that the court belonged to the third house, Beezy's childhood home: I'm sure of it. It's exactly the kind of nasty prank a house of ashes would pull—

And just like that the fever broke.

'Oh, Owen—'

Owen didn't try to clean himself off and he didn't try to hold Autumn's egg. He just walked off the court without looking at any of us and we knew, with a sudden spurt of nauseated release, that the game was over, love-all.

17. Intermezzo: Beatrice Danforth Lodge

I don't know what the lilac swing was in Beezy's book but here's how I imagine it:

At the end of a long, green garden, there is a swing. The swing has two holes drilled into the short end of each side and is strung through with rope, the yellow prickly kind that turns brown and then a sort of silky greyish-white in weather. This rope is yellow and the plank is unpainted and still has its neat edges. It's a swing at the beginning of its life and there is no wind at all. It's the swing Evelyn Southall wishes she'd had and, while she's ensconced in the tightly upholstered burgundy arms of the commuter rail, she looks out the window and thinks about how she would have painted the plank lilac with some leftover paint. Other times, she thinks about how her father had strung the swing up in a lilac bower and how she would release the scent of lilac every time her little back struck the bushes behind. It's a swing that belongs entirely to Evelyn Southall and, in her imagination, no other children play on it, and most certainly not her own children, because Evelyn Southall does not have children and, in fact, doesn't plan on having any. She doesn't want them. What she wants is to look out the window in between places and think about her swing, which is beholden to no one because she's made it up.

'Oh well, you know,' our parents would laugh, 'Beezy was Beezy.'

When they brought Beezy back from the hospital after her stroke, they lined the kids up in the living room of the childhood home and wheeled in a white-haired lady, and it took them a moment to recognise their mom. And when they realised, one by one, that this silent old woman was the self-same mother who could trim a storm jib in gale-force winds and had whipped their tender butts without pity or remorse, it was both the end and beginning of something for them, as it was the end and beginning of something for her.

Anyway, I think about the lilac swing a lot, especially now that I'm older and most of us have families and jobs of our own and our hopes and disappointments have just become features of our lives we can tour like those bodies at Pompeii. Because it must have been something Beezy thought was just great, the lilac swing. It must have been worth having. But I'll never know and my sneaking suspicion is that's the point – the lilac swing wasn't for us, or for our parents, and probably not even for Beezy anymore. It was for someone else.

If you really wanted to parse the look on our parents' faces when we asked about the world's rejection of Beezy's book, you could also say it was crosshatched with hurt and defiance. It makes me think of them in shorts with shining foreheads suspended around Beezy, who wasn't looking at them at all but always towards something else, and how the kindest thing they could do for her was to wink themselves out. Was to man the crank and shaft and reverse the celestial machine, disappearing one after the other in reverse order of birth until there weren't any of them left, and then Beezy would be free to be brilliant if not happy, a chloroplastic flowering of never-ending potential.

18. End of the Road

The hill dipped a last and final time and Autumn and Owen went ahead together, holding hands. We were right behind them, queasy with regret, but they seemed wholly alone. Just as if we didn't exist for them anymore. It was a sad feeling. The candy had liquified and no one could stomach looking at anyone else, so instead we called for Abi and Travis. After all, it's why we're there, we reminded each other sheepishly. Although we'd forgotten ourselves back on the court, right now we just needed Travis and Abi and to find our way home.

'Aaaa-beeee!'

Where there'd been pines, there were now giant, juicy deciduous trees, rhubarb, wild irises, stool-coloured leafmould, fungi, the whole forest swelling, thickening, passing us through. The smell from Owen's legs was highly putrid, but, despite the turd and the yolk, any one of us would have very gladly taken him in our arms in that moment. We would have been honoured, I imagine.

Our feet pulled us down the hill like lead weights at the end of a line.

'Come here, Owen,' we could have said, and then we would have wrapped ourselves around his little bones and held him in and no one would have needed to say that we were sorry.

'Traaaaa-vis! Aaa-beeeeee!'

'Owen—' one of us began, but then someone else said, 'Stop!', and we stopped and there it was.

A river is a feeling more than a sound. It makes an animal of you, is what I'm saying: you become the constituent parts, no more, no less. Some people may find relief in that but not me.

We heard it but actually we already knew.

The hill poured us forth: a long winding strip of open sky, frills of root-beer-coloured mud, rushes, the amplified sound of running water. The sun had fallen, its heat filtered through a jam cloth of ferment and insect life, and, although there weren't any bugs on this side of the river, not a bumblebee to be seen, nary a mosquito, their fanged and swampish vibe remained.

Only down to the river and along. Across the river the forest picked back up, carrying outwards and upwards and containing therein other houses and families and connecting roads, calm and sweet and well-ordered.

As for us, however, we'd reached the end of the road. In many ways we'd done our level best.

'Aaaa-beeee! Traaaa-vis!'

We stared at the opposite bank. It wasn't far, the length of three skipping ropes tied together. A squirrel ran up a tree, pausing midway and then disappearing into the canopy. A dragonfly rested nattily on a far-shore rock, then lifted away. One of us snapped a cattail and it sounded like a tree falling. *Timber!*

'They have to be back at the house. We need to go back up the hill,' one of the more reasonable cousins suggested.

The river wasn't wide but it was deep, the water very fast, tying and untying itself. Our sneakers made craters in the mud and the craters filled with water.

'Alright then, OK. But—'

Try looking at a fast-moving river for any real amount of time and see what happens. What happens is you start to worry about babies in baskets. Whether you'd fish one out.

'Let's go back and see. If we just walk back up—'

And you come to the conclusion that it depends on whether that baby had an aura of 'places to go, people to see', whether it was meant for greater things.

'Yeah, OK—'

But the more you think about it, the more you realise that actually a baby's sense of purpose is irrelevant. You wouldn't have any choice but to tow the basket to shore and place the baby into some kind of foster care situation because you'd never be able to explain that feeling to anyone. If you'd let the baby go its merry way, people would just think you were a lazy and uncaring monster who was possibly also afraid of water.

'OK, but, hey, Owen, um—'

And so because of you and your cowardly adherence to societal norms, that baby would grow up to pursue a degree in something like Computer Science instead of becoming God's lightning rod, and while that baby might be happier, the world would have lost out on something integral. That was a bad example.

Psychology maybe. Or Theatre Design.

We looked up at the bright blue sky and then down the long corridor that led towards town and then the sea and then the other way, deeper into the forest, and then on, I suppose, to the city. In order not to think about other things, we thought about babies and then we thought about children who might live on the other side of the river. We thought about providence and manifest destiny, though not in those words exactly. We looked at Autumn and Owen, though it was clear they didn't want to look at us.

We let our tired minds wander.

'Owen, listen. Owen, and Autumn too, look, we're really—'

What caught our eye in the end was his stripes, so bright they could have never belonged in nature. A wail broke loose, shaking cousin after cousin. Travis, just a few cousin-lengths away in the reeds, a dampened flare of engine red in all that hunting green, and the clean bright day pouring itself over what it had done.

19. Back

Because the Macalasters were gone by the time we made it up the gravel drive, we didn't get to see the ambulance sitting there amongst our parents' war animals. I imagine it with flashing lights and open doors. The jockey was there, though: he waved his lamp at us as we rounded the corner. It wasn't even on, that lamp, although it was basically early evening and, in fact, no one had ever put a candle in that jockey's lamp since time began. He'd never stood a chance.

They took Travis to the closest hospital and then on to a very fine one, where he turned thirteen. We brought him a foil helium balloon, which he couldn't really appreciate, but our parents assured us that it was the gesture that was important. For his fourteenth birthday I can't remember if we brought a balloon to the hospital or not.

We sat on Frankie's front steps and looked at the jockey. Our parents were gathering up our things inside, so we sat and looked, and Frankie came and sat with us and, for once in her life, she was dry-eyed because I guess her tears were mostly cheap and this wasn't one of those occasions. She lit a cigarette and only later did we think about the fact that Frankie didn't smoke. Frankie had long scratches on her legs and arms from ploughing through the brush. She closed her eyes and tilted her face up to the sky and let out a big white cloud, and the setting sun sat in her hair and lit it from within.

'Do you kids,' she croaked, 'want some cake?'

We shook our heads. We did not.

Frankie kept her eyes closed and nodded.

When she opened her eyes again she saw that we were looking at the jockey and she told us that it was Beezy's.

'That was your grandmother's,' she pointed with her cigarette. 'I painted it, though.'

Yes, yes, we nodded. We knew this already. We looked at his appalling face ratcheted forward on beseeching shoulders, and thought in a roundabout way about the person who had made it and the person who had wanted it made and the person who had decided to keep it and display it and pass it on, and though we probably didn't put it this way to ourselves in that moment, I think we could feel the ripple this rotten thing made, and that it would carry us along with it if we let it, which we probably would, not wanting to hurt anyone's feelings. We would let it pick us up and take us along and, really, if we had to, we could do touch-ups now and then with our own jar of pink paint and that would be fine.

Someone reached a hand out to touch him, to give him some reassurance maybe, but instead they ended up rapping the side of his head, right on his shiny pink temple. The hollowness of the whole thing made a kind of tonging noise, which felt bad for some reason. The jockey stared at us inanely so we looked away.

And the glutinous mantle beyond the drive? Gone

gone gone. As if it had never been there at all. Which it had, of course. Been there. That isn't in dispute.

The sun was dropping like a golden yolk and everywhere was violet: sky a light violet, the shadows at the treeline a dark violet, and even the air had a powdery violet finish. Mosquitoes floated around our heads.

A story: A couple years later our parents took what remained of us, with the exception of Autumn and Owen, to a Renaissance fair. We had little notion of what a Renaissance fair entailed and so we were taken by surprise to see adults roaming amongst the pines, tooting on horns and juggling fiery batons and lurching out to enquire whether you had 'a sixpence for a goodly fellow' and all that. We enjoyed it well enough and, in fact, it was pretty magical, and we took pictures of ourselves pilloried or with our heads stuck through boards painted up so that it looked like you were a jester throwing up balls that would never come down. Some of us had our own money and we bought things like malachites in suede pouches and wizard hats, which our parents complained were ahistorical. We ate sausages and drank lemonade.

The day was set to finish with a joust. It was the crown jewel of the fair and all anyone talked about in the hour or so leading up to it. You could feel its imminence moving through the crowds. Fifteen minutes before the gates opened to the specially constructed wooden arena, trumpets sounded.

'The joust!' we murmured. 'It's starting!'

The audience was divided into two. You couldn't

choose which side you were on, though I suppose they tried not to split up families because this was more or less before cell phones and otherwise you'd have to arrange to meet back at the car. Ours was the white knight. When our knight rode out on his horse, an employee in period dress ran up and down the bleachers encouraging us to holler but we needed no encouragement. We rose up and bellowed. Our collective voices were much deeper than any one of our voices could have been on its own. Our knight's horse was wearing a white blanket with red tassels and on our knight's shield there was a picture of a rose. He had yellow hair and a yellow beard and a large, symmetrical smile. What I'm saying is that he was very beautiful in a simple way that made him easy to like.

The other knight's colours were a less appealing combination, though I can't remember what exactly. When he rode out we booed, and even though the other side had been polite for our knight, it didn't matter. We clamoured and snarled.

Besides the horses' blankets and their shields, once they had their helmets on both knights looked more or less the same, though you could tell our knight was noble and the other knight was dastardly to the core. The other knight kept doing jerky things like starting before the signal and giving our knight a shove when his back was turned. He was really hamming it up and we liked jeering him almost as much as we liked cheering our own guy.

When our guy rode up to one of the fine ladies in the stalls and she proffered him a rose to match his shield, the other knight made a sort of la-di-da hand gesture inside his armour, which made us furious. Our knight didn't care. He had his lady's rose and rode in small circles holding it aloft, which, if not the picture of discretion, was a crowd-pleaser and we howled our pleasure.

In the final turn the knights faced each other. The sun, I remember, was low in the sky, very much the same time of day as it had been that afternoon on Frankie's front steps, the same hush and violet hue. It would be time to go home after this. The festival would be battened down for the night, velveteen tablecloths rolled up, tables folded, money put into lockboxes. We would fall asleep on the car ride home and our parents would lift the smallest amongst us out of the cars and gently prod the larger ones awake. But beforehand they would likely stop to marvel at our innocence. They would be reminded, I imagine, of Travis, and then put that thought away because there was nothing else to do with it.

The knights rode at each other hard because this was the show-down, you see; there was nothing after this, or that's what we thought, and so when our knight fell there was the silence of disbelief. We expected a team of paramedics to rush onto the scene, to peel him from his armour and ferry him away because surely this had to be a mistake, a horrible workplace accident. The other knight circled the body on his horse. It was only when he raised his metal glove above his head and four squire-ish men walked over with a wooden casket that we understood.

The squires lowered our knight's body into the casket

and then, using two sturdy poles, walked it with minimum ceremony onto a pallet set about with logs – what were we thinking of when they put out the pallet, and where had we been looking when they arranged all those logs? – and all the while the other knight was capering about on his horse, soaking up the boos that had begun to percolate in the dusk.

The squires retreated to the darkness of the stalls and returned with torches with long, bright tails, which they used to spring up the logs, and even though we knew our knight had scrabbled through some trapdoor or something, someone screamed. It could have been any of us kids, I suppose. The squires stepped back into the shadows and the flames flapped against the violet sky as the arena watched, stricken. The flames were many shades of orange and cream and would have been really something special if they hadn't wanted us also to imagine a body melting down at the centre of them. Some of us began to cry even though we knew it was all part of the show, and our parents put their arms around us and you could tell they were embarrassed for not knowing it was going to end like this, for not doing the correct amount of research.

'It's just a show,' they assured us, 'it's not real,' but we sensed that in some way we were being punished for having set our hearts on the wrong man. And not only were we being punished, but we were helping whoever was pulling the strings to finish him off, our lovely knight, we were letting it happen because it was part of the show and the show, ultimately, was for us.

Back on the steps, we looked away from the jockey to Frankie, who had finished her cigarette. The sun had lost its shape and was just a baggy bit of neon seeping over the location of the childhood home where the lady with the groceries would probably be making her family dinner or something equally inappropriate at a time like this. Frankie kept her eyes closed because, in this moment, being asleep was preferable to being awake, and tossed the butt far out into the garden where any old chicken could get at it.

20. Level 6

I don't know what Beezy was like as a child. No one does.

I imagine, though, that she was the sort of kid who liked asking questions she already knew the answer to and then not bothering to help you out as you floundered. I bet she could tie her shoes with one hand. You have to respect that kind of person even if you don't much like them.

I can't picture her, the child Beezy, in Frankie's house or in the childhood home for that matter, but I can absolutely picture her in the house made of ashes, wavering back there on its foundations in the resinous heart of our land, seeing without being seen. On her lilac swing, probably, thinking impassable thoughts. That's where she's at her cheeriest.

And what had Beezy seen down the hill at the river on that very bright and very clean June day? Because Travis was a top-tier swimmer, level 6, just two down from lifeguard. That was what the grownups kept saying, wouldn't *stop* saying, over the phone late at night or around kitchen tables, manning the crank shafts, the winch hooks, reversing, grinding the gears. And why in Christ's name was he wearing his *shoes* and how did *saltwater* make its way into his lungs, now how in the world could that be?

And while our guess was better than theirs, it still wasn't much.

It was Autumn, of course, who got there first. It took most of us to turn his long body over – after all he was the tallest and also the oldest, but also wet to the bone, and even though we had finally found him we called out his name. We beat his back with our fists, and all the time we called his name, and then Travis's chest rippled, it pulled outwards and a pailful of water spilled from his mouth and Autumn stood – she stood over us with her burnt face and scratched-up arms, her hair blocking out the sun, which was not hard; the sun was so distant, it had nothing to do with us anymore – Autumn stood, turned uphill, and ran.

It was both a long time and probably not long at all. Cradled on his side in the reeds, Travis looked just born, although we'd known him all our lives.

The forest stood back on its heels and the sound of the river weakened to near-silence and no one cried or said much that I can remember. What I do remember was the feeling of being on a train journey after you'd bought your ticket and chosen your seat and installed your luggage overhead and there were no more choices to be made. We waited and, once in a while, someone reached out and stroked Travis's muddy hair.

Then someone plucked something from the mud and it was Abi's hair thing, and so we just tucked it back in Travis's pocket. In the craterous landscape of our foot-prints, Travis looked like a spaceman who'd fallen down and was just regaining his steam.

'Look,' someone said, pointing to what looked like pawprints mixed in with our own, but no one did because no one wanted to.

We waited for a time and then, from the forest, they burst, our tardy *deus ex machina*s, Frankie first, and then Aunt Maureen, golden chariots wheeling down from the mountaintop. And then the uncles and then Pin, carrying Autumn and bringing up the rear, Autumn with her head lodged in the soft space above Pin's breast, Autumn's egg a miracle in her hand, a miracle we only discussed later in hushed tones, the survival of that single blue and perfect egg.

But Pin and Autumn were not the rear, no they were not, because there she was, like one of those debutantes in very long gloves, the ferns nodding open around her, shy as curtains. One of us claimed that she was carrying Cheez Balls balanced on a paper plate. Another was sure that her cast had disappeared, that her arm was whole and strong. All of us agree, however, that she was soaking wet, her pigtails poured into dark, hard spirals, and at the root of each pigtail, a pair of bright pink plastic stars. She was wet head to toe and the look she gave us remains unclear. I'm really not able to describe it at all except to say that it was very distant, as if she were looking down on us from a great height rather than a few feet up a muddy slope. Abi, elegant almost, ancient-seeming, light as anything.

21. Intermezzo: Palaces

After all that, it wasn't the *Winter* but the *Alexander* Palace where the Romanovs lived. I'm sorry, I didn't know that but now I do. I looked it up and they didn't spend much time at the Winter Palace – it was overlarge, historians think, and too much at the crux.

The Alexander Palace, on the other hand, was smaller and tucked away, with lots of areas of interest so you'd never need to leave. In addition to an Elephant House and a Children's Island, they installed electric wires under the silk wallpaper and a man in the basement for phone calls and, all in all, it was very cosy.

The family liked it so much that Peter Fabergé made one of his eggs about it, with pictures of the kids and a tiny replica of the palace and grounds. It was a gift for the mother but got pinched by those Bolsheviks, and then Peter Fabergé died of a broken heart. The Bolsheviks had traversed the boundary, you see, and then it was over.

They'd just walked through it like it was nothing.

I've seen photos of the egg. It's gold-and-green enamel with garlands of diamonds and rubies, and while you'd think you'd open the house to find the kids inside, it's actually the other way round – the house is inside the kids, which must be, I suspect, how the mother had wanted it all along.

22. Finale

At the beginning, Frankie's house was just a large square hole with concrete walls and long bundles of two-by-fours. In my memory of it, the sky is low and the colour of old rope and creaking with the possibility of heavy, sudden rain, and Frankie is there in her shorts with a pencil behind her ear, working away. Building her house and very happy, because she liked work of all kinds. Also because the Mechanic is just on his way, you can feel him at the edges, empty-handed but ready to help where he can; we liked him a lot, we really did. And it's the sort of day where everything is happening on-stage and nothing else really matters except what you have in front of you: things that are new and right-angled and measured down to the millimetre and need to be used in a very particular order and, if you want something, just hop in your car and go to Home Depot.

I imagine this would have been around the time that the Mechanic showed some of us the Big Dipper on the hood of Frankie's car, so that means Frankie would have forgotten to return us before dinnertime. On the way home she would have made a pit stop at Dairy Queen so we couldn't say she hadn't fed us and, before we went inside to our parents, she would have told us we'd been a terrific help, and although we'd probably spent most of the day accruing minor injuries and misplacing key items, we would have felt this to be true. Frankie's house was a house of the future and it was fun walking around going, 'Here is the kitchen, here is the window and here is the door.'

It was our house then, I think, more than it is now.

Anyway, Abi went to Travis's lovely school when she turned five. Despite his crimes, the school felt bad about what happened to Travis, so they gave Abi a partial scholarship, which was generous and also better than nothing. By that point Uncle Steve was back at work and it was a real balm to have all those things for Abi – the counselling and studio time and enviable student/ teacher ratios – because Aunt Maureen had her hands full with catheters and unguents and also opening and closing the shades.

Here's a photo of Abi on her first day, standing at her front door. Little Abi, looking away from the camera off to the side, as if someone who was not the photographer was calling her name, and above her head the wreath Aunt Maureen hung up every September: dried white grasses and papery colourless flowers spraying out from her head like a supernova.

For us, however, Abi was up next to Beezy on the already crowded display shelf of grievous inconsistencies. Because it doesn't matter how many times we told our parents we'd been looking for her – they insisted each time that Abi was *right there, on the deck, she was with them the whole time*. We didn't bother to ask why, if she'd been at their side eating Cheez Balls and being a charming nuisance, she'd been wet as a newborn calf, because they had always moved on by then: the shoes, the saltwater, the shock of the thing, the inconceivable unfairness of it all, cogs meeting, locking, turning overhead in scintillating formations until the end of our days.

Here is Abi looking down a wooded hill from the window of a long-ago house.

Here is Abi being hailed across a fast, black river like she's a taxi with something waiting impatiently on the other side, something whose calls were more inexorable than our own: zip zip zip!

And here is Travis, seeing her wade in to the waist of her tiny underpants and Travis running down and down the hill and throwing himself in after her. Only Travis doesn't know that he's blown it, you see, he doesn't know that *Abi* is now the baby in the basket and that he, in the grand scheme of things, is *squat*.

And so whereas some of us became teachers and custodians and technical directors and parents in our own right, Abi became an artist, exceedingly celebrated, just as we'd always known/feared she would.

Here is Abi accepting an award of some sort at a glass podium with her hair balanced on her head like a forgotten bowl of fruit.

Here is Abi in a man's button-down shirt, looking out from next to an ad for the Mandarin Oriental Hotel. The expression on Abi's face is this: timeless equipoise.

Here is Abi on the lilac swing and here is someone pushing her with great force.

If you're at all interested, you can see Abi the artist's

quilts in Bilbao and New York and Seoul and online and many other places. Abi the artist has only ever done the one thing, though what that is only she could really tell you: beyond the fact that the quilts are greenish and implacable and you really wouldn't want one on your bed, I have nothing more to add. We've not seen Abi the girl in years and years.

As for Autumn and Owen, you can't claim they weren't civil. I suppose Pin, despite predictions to the contrary, had raised them well, so whenever we saw them at future gatherings, Autumn always waved at us before she turned away to get someone a drink or some other ostentatiously helpful thing, her leg stiff as a wood post. Autumn who ran and lost class president three times on the same platform with the same amount of goodwill and went on to have two kids: one lumbering, dark-haired boy, one scribble of a girl.

And Owen who doted on his niece and nephew badly, with them for every Christmas and birthday and Thanksgiving, spending all the metaphorical pennies of an otherwise scant life on those kids. They were so gentle with him, you should have seen it.

But although Owen was a faultless uncle, he was, after that June afternoon, an indifferent cousin. After that day, Owen didn't have a single cent for us. In the end we were just an empty voice calling his name while he went about the poor business of a life without us – us, who loved him best of all but no longer counted. Owen.

Frankie, on the other hand, is still Frankie.

The Thanksgiving after the birthday party, some of

us gathered at Frankie's and although the mince pie was in attendance, the other main players were not. Aunt Maureen and her lot were at the hospital with Travis, and Autumn and Owen went finally to visit Carl, which everyone had mixed but hopeful feelings about, while Pin stayed home to have some peace. So it was just us and Frankie and our parents, on their best behaviour, and the house, of course. Because it was November, we ate inside around Frankie's long dining-room table and she had even lit candles in pewter sticks, and it was nice, actually, to see the little flames and their darting fish-like shadows. We all held hands and said grace, which really was a first, and the looming blooms had retreated behind their bars, the majolica was shut up in its cupboard. There was a turkey and the usual selection of potatoes and things, and this time some thought had been given to the children, so horseradish was at an absolute minimum and there was Coke and an apple pie. Because Travis was the obvious thing to talk about, he'd been talked about already every single minute of every day, and so they decided for once to give it a rest and instead the conversation was effervescent and without import.

When evening started in and the grownups pulled back their chairs to help clear and wash up and tidy away, Frankie made her exit to muck out the stalls and stable the horses. With not much to do except get in their way, our parents, who would never let us out of their sight again, not in any really meaningful way, suggested we join her but warned us to stick together and all that sort of thing, and we agreed.

We put on our coats and shoes and hats and mittens and we followed Frankie's trail out into the damp, mineral chill, and the dark was lovely and calm after the lights and clamour inside. It was nice not to be able to see much, which is the opposite, of course, to how it usually is. An uncle's silhouette watched us from the window and we waved back.

We didn't look left or right but just followed the steps under the deck and into the black square of the open barn door. Frankie had turned on the fake oil lamp in the office and it cast a large yellow coin of light onto the floor. We could hear her out at the paddock gate in the dark and her voice was like our moms' voices when we were just babies, and it was both soothing and strange to think of her that way.

As we passed Beezy's photo on our way up, she wasn't looking at us but instead had relaxed back into the scene with her children, her pets, the childhood home, wherever it was, everything in its place.

The loft was even larger in the dark, as large as we wanted it to be, only as small as the limits of our imagination. When one of us found the light switch, we were all incredibly relieved to not be responsible anymore for determining the size and shape of our surroundings. Nothing had changed as far as we could see. We pottered, picking things up and putting them down again: books, a loafer, a three-pronged gardening fork. A box full of red and green and blue ribbons, only these ones were for things like Best Bitch, which we thought was very splendid but only in principle, because Frankie didn't *have* dogs. It's possible I forgot to mention that before.

We moved on: a framed print of an empty landscape, a shoebox of receipts, the red accordion file, its contents dull except for the one thing. It wasn't bound like a book after all but instead held together with plastic teeth, its cover the antique yellow of flypaper. I pulled it out and sat with it on a bale. *The Lilac Swing.* On the front, Beezy had made Frankie type *Beatrice* and then her maiden name – *Danforth Lodge* – which was a little mortifying, like catching someone trying on underwear over their clothes. There wasn't any dedication but there was a bit from Frankie's poem 'The Charge of the Light Brigade': *Pa*-pa pa-*pa* pa-*pa boldly we rode and well.* I'd like to think that Frankie snuck it in because she couldn't help herself, but I doubt it; Beezy must have liked that poem too. I skimmed the first chapter while Frankie moved around below our feet, the scrape of the shovel on the stall floor, the sigh of the feed bin on its hinges, then I put it away. I imagine it's still there. You could read it too if you wanted. You could swing by any time.

Out the barn window above the plateau of hay bales, the bright rectangles of Frankie's house showed our parents at the sink, opening cupboards, slinging dishrags, saying things over their shoulders, drawing things to a close, and beyond that the paddock, the woods, and the river. Everything except for those bright rectangles was tamped down with shadow, and stars were beginning to show through – pale stars, the first ones who like to stick their neck out. The others padded carefully around the hatch and Frankie crooned to the horses in the darkness below, speaking to them so softly all the words ran together into one continuous word and all we could pick out were nursery ones, like *fishies* and *dishies*. She spoke so gently we forgot about the horses' fiendish ability to transmogrify and injure and just thought about their cloth-like noses, the way they folded themselves down to sleep, all their special things wiped and polished and hung up just so. Frankie susurrated and moved with great care.

'Hey!' It was a larger cousin, an also-ran. 'Look at this.'

The address book lay open on the workbench and in the cousin's hand a thin sheaf of photos, with some more spread across the surface between spare circular saw blades.

Some of the photos were of our parents when they were children:

The uncles in Elmer Fudd hats in a world of greyish snow.

Pin and Frankie in front of a Christmas tree, in colour, each one holding out a large, hard-headed doll. Pin a bit meh, Frankie in fits of ecstasy.

A teenage Aunt Maureen looking up from a desk beside an open window, tweedy and exasperated.

There were some of people we didn't know. Frankie's friends, maybe: the repellent horse people with their popped collars, sunning themselves on her deck.

And one, of course, of Beezy. We might have even seen it first or we could have seen it somewhere in the middle, but in my memory it comes last, like all the others were just her cortège but in reverse. It was a mate to the picture downstairs, a second in a series of I don't know how many, but there were only two left so they formed a pair: one holding the hand of the other, providing, I imagine, some level of familiarity if not comfort.

It was, simply, Beezy without children.

That's all.

Our parents hadn't been called down yet or else they'd been dispersed, so Beezy was alone on the front steps of our parents' childhood home, and this time she was looking neither left nor right and the flash of the camera had bounced off the glass of the front door and so, behind her, you couldn't see very much, just a blazing white stain and Beezy, legs tucked and hair rolled, looking down the barrel of the camera, smiling and singular.

It was another clue, but the mystery was over and we were tired. To put it frankly, we weren't up to it. So we put the photo back and the other photos too, and we shrugged at each other and thought that this was the end of the line in terms of the evening, which was fine. We just wanted to go home now.

'Let's throw hay down the hatch,' someone suggested, a last hurrah, and we thought *why not*. It was a fantastic idea actually. A firework of hay to mark the occasion.

We walked to the edge of the hatch and called down.

'Frankie!' we called. 'We're going to throw hay down the hatch!'

We waited for her to signal her approval but she hadn't heard us. Frankie's murmuring continued as she made things right downstairs.

'Frankie!' we called, but it was no use. So we each took a handful of hay and we tossed it down the hatch and it spiralled nicely against the dark, so we did a bit more.

'Frankie!' we yelled. 'It's snowing!'

Frankie's murmuring rose in volume, just a little, it crept up in its pace.

'Merry Christmas, Frankie!' we screamed, throwing armfuls down, and the murmuring below slipped into a higher gear, shushing, supplicating, and we went back to the bales for more, more and more, and that's when we saw them through the window: two of them at the paddock gate under the watery light of the moon. Bloadie and Ondin not in their stalls at all. Blondin and Oadie not bedding down for the night below, but perched on their precarious, murderous stilts, peering up the hill at us, curious, maybe, about these shadows moving past the lit window of their home. Zip zip zip. We looked down the hatch where Frankie's murmuring continued like a generator and – *nostra sponte* – we burst. The first shoe went down the hatch, and the second, the bag of decorations in a loose shower of glitter, and then the shirts, first one, then all of them, ripped off their hangers, twisting and filling with air, and if we could have we would have thrown more – the statue, the jockey, the majolica – in the grip of our horrors we would have thrown everything, that bright and clean day, and all the things we'd failed to do, the things that were travelling towards us at an undetermined speed with only the fact of their arrival certain, and Frankie's moaning became an entreaty and we became an ear that could or would not hear it.

And then the ribbons, and those were wonderful to throw, like something you'd throw at a wedding or a funeral, so we threw those down and then the photos, down, down, down. And though I didn't see it go, I imagine that Beezy's photo went down. I imagine her face was a narrow beam of light disappearing into the darkened hatch – only this time Frankie was down there with her rather than up on deck, saying all the goodbye things Beezy must have only half-listened to, impatient as she was to be on her way: *we love you, we'll miss you, old gal* and all that silly rubbish, maybe even a salute – it was Frankie after all. I imagine Frankie standing on the shore as the sailboat's engine came to life and it motored away from the dock for the very last time, radiant, hell-bent, good money after bad, and Frankie's shining forehead was whatever the opposite of a beacon might be.

'What on God's green earth could she have possibly said to you,' Aunt Maureen had asked Frankie on that other Thanksgiving, the Year of the Slap, 'to make you help her do that?'

Everyone had gone very quiet. Us, the cousins, in front of the fire with our chocolate birds and milk-coloured stones, the adults spread out around the room on settees and wingbacks, locked into doorways, hands frozen above piano keys.

Frankie had looked at us just then, the cousins, and her face was stretched into a funny kind of rapture.

'Oh, you know,' Frankie told us, 'you know,' quivering with happiness, 'she really didn't have to say much at all.'

And then Frankie got into her convertible alone and drove herself home and stayed that way for ever, except, of course, for whatever was down there with her now in the black of the barn.

Oh, Frankie. Down and down and down, until we grew tired and we all just sat around the hatch like rock formations on the Earth's surface, which would have made Frankie and her pets the substratum, I guess, and then below them the family land and its bag of tricks, which was, if I'm to push this metaphor past its natural limits, the core.

We were all quiet now, even Frankie.

We were absolutely spent.

Our parents weren't happy when they came to look for us.

Time's up, they called, and *what's all this*, but in the end they gave us a pass, feeling, I think, on some level that they had failed us again, just as we'd failed ourselves. We came down at the sound of their voices; we were tired and we wanted to go home more than we were afraid of what we had done. And there was Frankie, sitting against the wall of the stall, and the wrack line of old shit washed against her sneakers, the shirts, the glitter, the photos, the ribbons, our inheritance, all of it, mostly all. And Frankie was smiling. She held her arms open.

'Kids.'

'Goodnight, Frankie,' we said, and we kissed her on the cheek, one by one, and she looked shy and pleased, even, that we had kissed her after throwing things down on her head.

'Goodnight, you kids,' she told us. 'Come back soon.'

And so we took our parents' hands and re-entered the evening. We crossed the blue-gravel drive and withdrew ourselves one by one. And then we fastened our seat-belts and under a sky that I hope you can see was simply ridden with stars, we turned our horses towards the future.

Acknowledgements

Thank you to my agent Daisy Chandley, for being the best spirit guide a book could ask for.

To my editors Linda Mohamed and Sally Howe, for attending with such unbelievable care to the head and heart of the book. And to all the other wonderful people at Hutchinson Heinemann, Scribner and Peters Fraser + Dunlop who helped it on its way: Rebecca Wearmouth, Madison Thân, Cameron Watson, Hana Sparkes, Joanna Taylor, Anna Hervé, Sarah-Jane Forder, Lauren Dooley, Kassandra Rhoads, Dan Simpkins, Tristan Offit, Annette Sweeney and Stephanie Evans.

A special thank you to my teachers, Don Paterson, Jacob Polley, Emily Fragos, Gerry Cambridge, Alex Thomson, Kate Seward and Kazim Ali. In particular to Dr Richard Ladd, who taught high school like it mattered. Also to Jane Commane at Nine Arches Press and the excellent folk at the Scottish Book Trust for your much-valued support.

My unending gratitude to all the friends who read this book and other work when it was only half-dressed, or gave encouragement when it was most needed: Liz Hurst-High, Kirsty Wilson, Ellie Bush, Jennie Baker, Kamili Posey, Sean Macleod, Ryan Van Winkle, Nick Holdstock, Thom Laycock, Annie McCrae, Tina Norris, Geraldine Gould and Fiona Forsyth.

Thank you to my talented work-wife, Jane Fox, for her patience, taste and wisdom. And to Adeline Amar, whom I love and who has been with me this whole time.

To my family: my little sisters across the street, Siv Brun Lie and Cecelia Lie-Spahn, Debbie Socolar and Bob Bamford for always sending the best books, the Gows for being such a warm and welcoming clan, and Jill Gleim, who takes childhood seriously. To the Royers, especially Mamie. To my aunts, Sandra, Sheila, Dedi and Tracy, and my grandmother, Johanne, the opposite of Beezy in every way that counts.

To my brilliant sister, Emilie Wyatt – who's lived all of this – and her wonderful family.

To my amazing kids, Marianne and Ben, for taking occasional pity on me and my pleas for 'just five minutes'.

To my mom. Because obviously.

And to David, my bidie-in: it's the privilege of my life.